ABERDEENSHIRE LIBRARY
AND INFORMATION SERVICE
ME| Patino, Ernesto |RUM

In the shadow
of a stranger /
Ernesto Patino
            F LP

1234863

D1349991

1234863

Ernesto Patino grew up in El Paso, Texas, and worked for 23 years as an FBI agent. He lives in Miami, Florida. *In the Shadow of a Stranger* is his first novel.

IN THE SHADOW OF A STRANGER

As a result of a chance encounter with a Holocaust survivor on vacation in Mexico City, young attorney Antonio de la Vega learns that his natural father is a former SS officer who committed heinous crimes against the Jews during World War II. Obsessed with the idea of meeting his father, Antonio embarks on a search that takes him from Mexico to the United States and ultimately to South America, meeting ageing ex-Nazis, vindictive Jews, and an alluring young woman who has been assigned to watch his every move. Meanwhile, Antonio's semi-recluse mother is suddenly faced with the possibility that the man she once loved may soon reappear . . .

ERNESTO PATINO

IN THE SHADOW OF A STRANGER

Complete and Unabridged

ULVERSCROFT
Leicester

First published in Great Britain in 2001 by
Robert Hale Limited
London

First Large Print Edition
published 2002
by arrangement with
Robert Hale Limited
London

British Library CIP Data

Patino, Ernesto
   In the shadow of a stranger.—Large print ed.—
Ulverscroft large print series:
   1. Fathers and sons—Psychology—Fiction
   2. War criminals—Fiction
   3. South America—Fiction
   4. Suspense fiction 5. Large type books
   I. Title
813.6 [F]

ISBN 0–7089–4674–7

Published by
F. A. Thorpe (Publishing) Ltd.
Anstey, Leicestershire

Set by Words & Graphics Ltd.
Anstey, Leicestershire
Printed and bound in Great Britain by
T. J. International Ltd., Padstow, Cornwall

This book is printed on acid-free paper

For Diana

1

Mexico City, 1985

'I think I'm going to have something light,' Betty said from across their table in the middle of the patio. 'Maybe a cup of soup with a side order of guacamole.'

Harry wasn't really listening. Without bothering to look up as he pored over the menu, he said, 'What are you going to have, honey?'

After a few moments, he put down his menu. 'I hope the food here isn't too spicy. You know how my stomach gets whenever . . . ' He glanced across the courtyard and saw a tall, young man walk in and take a seat at a corner table. A second later a smiling waiter rushed over to greet him.

'It's him. It's him,' Harry said, trying to contain himself.

'What are you talking about?' Betty said, turning to look in the direction of Harry's gaze. 'You look as though you've seen a ghost.'

'It's him, I tell you. The man who killed my family.'

'The Nazi? You can't be serious. That's a young man.'

'No, No,' he said, almost shouting. 'The face. It's the same face, maybe forty years younger, but it's the same face. I wonder if — '

'Put it out of your mind,' Betty said. 'The young man is probably not even German. Besides, how can you recall what he looked like after all these years?'

His jaw muscles tightened. 'I'll never forget that face. Never, not as long as I live.'

Harry's mind raced back to 1941. He was standing naked in front of a long trench, alongside his sister, their parents and many other Jews who had been selected to die that day.

There were three of them, two corporals and a young, intense-looking SS officer who couldn't have been more than twenty-two or twenty-three years old. The two corporals took turns as they walked up to each person and pointed a pistol to their head. They fired once, sometimes twice, and the limp, nude bodies slumped down into the trench. His sister, beautiful and well-endowed, rushed up to the SS officer and pleaded for her life. The officer looked at her, totally unmoved by her pleas or the sight of her body. Without a word, he pulled out his Luger and shot her through the heart. He then walked up to Harry's parents and shot them, first his mother, then his father. And then it was his turn. He turned his head for a brief second and saw the SS officer's face clearly — cold blue eyes set into a thin, angular face with a strong jawline and a smallish, slightly upturned nose. The only thought that ran through his mind was that he wanted it to be over quickly. The young officer ordered him to turn his head towards the open trench. Suddenly there was a sound of gunshot, and he fell into the trench atop a heap of lifeless bodies. He lay there motionless, afraid to open his eyes, afraid to believe that, miraculously, the bullet had not penetrated his brain. The sound of gunshots continued until not a single Jew remained standing.

'It's in the past, Harry,' Betty said softly. She reached across the table and squeezed his hand gently to let him know she understood. 'There's nothing you can do to change what happened.'

'You're right,' he said unconvincingly. 'It's been too many years and my memory is not what it used to be. I guess I've gotten myself worked up over nothing.' He decided it would serve no purpose if he allowed his feelings to dominate his behavior during the few days they would spend in Mexico City. Betty had looked forward to the trip for months and he didn't want to do anything that would spoil it for her. Yet he couldn't get the young man's face out of his mind, and he knew that somehow he would have to find out more about him, if only to convince himself that he was just what he appeared to be. Someone who bore a remarkable resemblance to the SS officer from his past.

* * *

After lunch, they took a stroll through Alameda Park nearby and returned two hours later just as a group of tourists was being dropped off.

'Why don't you go up to the room while I sign us up for the pyramid tour?' Harry said, almost casually.

'That's a good idea. But don't take too long. We've got to get dressed to go to the folkloric ballet.'

Harry waited until he was sure Betty was back in the room before he went to the courtyard to look for the waiter from earlier in the day. He spotted him standing next to a fountain.

'Excuse me,' Harry said. 'I wonder if you can help me.'

'But of course,' the waiter responded.

'Earlier in the day my wife and I were sitting in the courtyard and I spotted someone that I thought I recognized. He was a tall, young man, about thirty, thirty-one years old, wearing a light gray suit, and he sat over there at that table.' He pointed to a corner table near the entrance. 'Can you tell me anything about him? I got the impression he was a regular customer.'

The waiter took a moment to think. 'I know who you're talking about,' he said, finally. 'His name is Antonio de la Vega. He's an attorney and he comes here for lunch, maybe two, three times a week.'

'Well, actually I think I was mistaken,' Harry said. 'The person I thought I recognized was definitely not Mexican. Thank you. Thank you very much.'

Harry walked away, completely engrossed in what the waiter had said. He decided that at the first opportunity, he would approach Mr de la Vega and introduce himself.

'Well, how did you make out?' Betty asked the moment he walked in the door. 'Are we signed up?'

He had forgotten about the pyramids. 'Uh . . . I didn't get a chance to inquire about it. The young man behind the counter suddenly became busy answering all kinds of phone calls. But don't worry, we'll have plenty of time to sign up early in the morning before breakfast. I understand the tour doesn't leave until nine or so.'

★ ★ ★

The next day Harry got up and dressed earlier than usual. He wanted to make sure the pyramid tour was still open.

Leaving his room, he ran into a boy mopping down the walkway and he paused. 'I wonder if you can do something for me,' he said. 'See that table over there?' He pointed down to the corner table in the courtyard. 'There's a young man who comes in to eat, maybe two or three times a week. He's Mexican but he looks American . . . gringo, you know? His name is Antonio de la Vega and he — '

'Señor de la Vega. Yes, I know who you're talking about. Everybody at the hotel knows Señor de la Vega. He's a very nice man.'

'Well, listen. I want you to do me a favor. Next time he comes in, let me know. You see, he's someone that looks like . . . well, never mind. Just knock on my door if you see him, okay?'

'Sí señor,' the boy said. 'I will let you know the moment I see him.'

Harry made his way down the stairway and

went straight to the lobby. A young man named Luis, who had greeted them upon their arrival, was standing behind the front desk.

'Good morning,' Harry said. 'I'd like to sign up for the pyramid tour.'

'I'm sorry, but it's all booked up,' Luis said. 'It's one of our most popular tours. Perhaps you and your wife would like to see something else. How about a bullfight?'

'A bullfight? Hmm . . . I don't know . . . '

'It's not until four in the afternoon, though. You can take a taxi from right in front of the hotel.'

'It would be something different, wouldn't it? Thanks, thanks a lot.' Harry walked away and returned to the room.

'The tour was all booked up, honey. I guess I should've got the tickets last night like I meant to do. The young man at the front desk suggested a bullfight. It's not until four this afternoon and this'll give us some time to do a little shopping. How does that sound?'

She thought about it for a second. 'I do need to buy a few things. But the bullfight . . . well, maybe it won't be so bad.'

2

The second bull of the day was jet black, with powerful shoulders that made his horns appear too small for his body. He raced around the ring furiously, trying to find a target. He saw none and so charged wildly at his own shadow. Suddenly he stopped and positioned himself in the center of the ring.

Two of the matador's helpers, a tall thin one and a short one of average build, rushed into the ring to test him, to see how he charged, to see if he favored his right or his left horn. They waved large capes to get his attention. They called out to him and jumped up and down, all to no avail. The bull refused to charge.

The tall helper slowly made his way towards the bull. He was within ten paces when it suddenly charged at his cape with such speed that it knocked the cape from out of his hands, causing him to stumble and fall. Before he had a chance to pick himself up, the animal swung around and charged directly at him. The bull's left horn caught him in the lower right thigh. The man lay helpless as the bull continued to drive the horn deeper into the thigh. The matador and other assistants quickly rushed to his aid and managed to distract the bull away from the injured helper. At the same time, other attendants acted swiftly to carry the man to a nearby infirmary.

Despite the goring, the bullfight continued.

'Let's get out of here, Harry,' Betty said.

Harry offered no objections. They got up from their seats and made their way down a steep stairway that led to a walkway. They were almost at the walkway when Harry looked across the rows of people directly to his left and spotted a young man who looked like Antonio. He was some distance away, at least twenty metres, and Harry was not really certain it was him. As they reached the walkway, Harry said to Betty, 'Give me a couple of seconds. I want to take a few shots of the bull. I really didn't get a chance before. From this distance I should be able to get some great pictures.' He adjusted his lens and began to snap one shot after another.

Harry inched his way towards the left to get a closer look at the young man, pretending as he went along to be snapping photographs of the bullfight. When he got close enough he looked up over four rows of spectators and quickly snapped a picture. For a second, Harry met Antonio's eyes. Their gaze was broken when crowds of spectators suddenly jumped to their feet amidst a swell of cheers as the matador completed a series of passes.

★   ★   ★

The next day Harry answered an unexpected knock at the door. It was the young boy with the mop.

'You wanted me to let you know when Señor de la Vega was on the patio,' he said. 'He got here a few minutes ago.'

'Thanks,' Harry said, trying to keep his voice down. He gave the boy a generous tip and quickly shut the door.

'Who was that, Harry?' Betty asked.

'Oh, it was just the maid. She . . . she wanted to know if we needed some extra towels. Listen, why don't you turn on the TV and see if there's something interesting while I go downstairs to get us a couple of beers. I'll be right back.'

'But Harry . . . ' The door shut behind him.

Harry stopped midway down the stairway to collect his thoughts. He took a deep breath, then continued down and walked right up to Antonio.

'Excuse me,' he said, nervously. 'My name

10

is Harry Friedman. I wonder if I can have a moment of your time. The other day my wife and I were sitting at that table over there.' He pointed. 'And when I saw you come into the courtyard I told my wife how much I thought you looked like . . . like someone I met in Poland many years ago. My wife said that I was probably mistaken and that — '

'Haven't we met before?' Antonio said. He looked stiff and uncomfortable in a double-breasted blue suit with a red tie and matching breast pocket handkerchief. 'The bullfight. Yes, it was yesterday at the bullfight. You were the one with the camera.'

'Yes, it was me,' Friedman said, nodding. 'May I sit down?' He seated himself before Antonio had a chance to respond. 'I promise I'll clear up any questions you have. The fact of the matter is, just by pure chance I recognized you as we were leaving the bullring. I really wasn't thinking when I took the picture. You see, ever since I first saw you, I have been wanting to meet you.'

'But why?'

'Well, like I started to say, you resemble someone that I met in Poland many years ago, over forty years, in fact. I know what you're thinking, but let me explain. I just thought that perhaps — and this is maybe going to sound a little crazy — that perhaps you are a relative of that person.'

'But I am not even Polish,' Antonio said. 'And my entire family has always lived in Mexico.'

'Oh, but the person I met in Poland was not Polish. He was . . . German.' He paused. 'It was shortly after the Germans had occupied Poland. The person I'm talking about was a young German officer. I saw him only once but I can assure you his face is one I will never forget. That's why when I first saw you here two days ago, I was completely stunned. You look exactly like him. Your hair, your eyes, the contour of your nose. The resemblance is incredible. I don't mean to pry into your personal life, but may I ask if any member of your family is of German descent?'

Amused, Antonio smiled and said, 'I'm sorry to disappoint you, but my family is Mexican one hundred per cent. My mother's family has been in Mexico for generations and my father, well, he died when I was very young. But his family came from Spain over two hundred years ago. So tell me, who was this person that I'm supposed to resemble, and how can you still remember what he looked like after all these years if, as you say, you saw him only once?'

Harry had not anticipated he would have to

provide the details surrounding that horrible day in Poland. He hesitated.

'First of all,' Harry said. 'Let me say that you have been very understanding about this and I'm sure someone else probably would've told me to buzz off. You deserve to know what this is all about. You see, that . . . person you happen to resemble so much is the man responsible for the murder of my family. It happened in front of my own eyes. My mother, my father, my sister and many other people. They were all murdered that day. I, too, should have died, but for some reason — and God only knows — I survived. On that day, just as the SS officer was about to put a bullet in my head, I turned around and saw his face. It was a quick glance but his features have stayed with me all these years. Believe me, his face can never be erased from my mind.'

Antonio nodded sympathetically.

'Once I left Poland, I heard nothing more about him and for all I know he may even be dead now,' Friedman said. 'I never got to know his name or anything about him. At the time I was just thankful to be alive.'

Harry saw the waiter walking towards them, carrying a tray with a basket of rolls and a glass of sherry. 'Well, I don't want to take up any more of your time,' he said. 'After

13

what you've told me, I'm convinced that it's just a coincidence.'

'I understand,' Antonio said. 'Were I in your position, I probably would've done the same thing. I must say though, it's a little disturbing to know I resemble someone so evil. But enough of that. Would you care to join me for lunch or maybe a glass of sherry?'

'Thank you, but I told my wife I was going downstairs to get us a couple of beers. She's probably wondering what happened to me.' He stood up and reached to shake the man's hand.

★　★　★

She was a petite woman, with light green eyes and soft brown hair tied back in a twist. As she was accustomed to doing whenever her son dropped by to visit, Mrs de la Vega reached into the china cabinet and picked up a decanter of sherry and a single glass, and brought them over to a table in front of the couch.

'By the way,' Antonio said as his mother began to pour, 'an interesting thing happened to me this afternoon. This old man came up to me as I was having lunch at the Hotel de Cortez. He told me the most incredible thing. He said I looked exactly like this German

14

officer who had killed his family in Poland during the war. He asked if any of my relatives were of German descent. I think he thought — '

She suddenly lost her grip on the decanter and spilled the sherry all over the table.

'Mother, are you all right?'

'I'm all right,' she said, her voice tense. 'It must be that medication Doctor Pacheco gave me for my high blood pressure. Here, let me finish pouring you some sherry. I'll have to get a cloth to clean the table. I'll be right back.'

She went straight to her bedroom and closed the door behind her. Her hands were trembling and the perspiration from her forehead was beginning to show through her make-up. Quickly, she retouched her face, picked up a towel and returned to the living room.

'Are you sure you're all right?' Antonio asked as she began to wipe up the spilled sherry.

'I'm all right, really,' she responded. She took the towel to the kitchen, then returned and walked over to the china cabinet to get a glass for herself. 'I think I'll join you. It'll do me good to relax before going to bed.' She poured herself some and sat down on the couch. 'Why don't you finish telling me about this man you met?'

'Well, there really isn't much more to tell. Like I said, he seemed curious to find out if I had any German blood in my background. He was just so amazed that I looked like — '

'But who was this man?' she asked. 'Had you met him before? Surely a stranger wouldn't have come up to you like that. I hope you told him it really wasn't any of his business. I mean ... it just isn't good manners to pry into a person's family the way he did.'

'I never met him before in my life. He was just an old man who apparently had gone through a tremendous ordeal during the war. He wanted to satisfy his curiosity, that's all. Actually, he seemed like a very nice person and I saw no reason not to answer his questions. I assured him that our family was all Mexican. Of course, once I told him about my father — '

'You told him about your father?' she said sharply.

He reached over to pour himself some more sherry. 'Yes, I told him he had died when I was very young and that his family had come from Spain over two hundred years ago. Well, anyway, by the time our conversation ended, he seemed satisfied that my resemblance to the German officer was just a coincidence. Afterwards, though, I thought about it, and the whole thing gave me the chills. To know that I resemble someone who committed such horrible crimes, well . . . '

'Do you think the old man will want to talk to you again?' she asked.

'I doubt it. Besides, he's a tourist and after a few days he'll leave Mexico City to return home. But why do you ask?'

She picked up her glass and took a quick sip. 'No reason.' She glanced at the clock on the wall. 'Oh, look at the hour. I didn't realize it was so late. I think I'll call it a night. Do you mind?'

'Of course not. I think I'll do the same. I've got a big meeting tomorrow morning with a client from Nuevo Laredo. You know how punctual those border people are. When they say nine-thirty, they mean nine-thirty.'

3

Three days after their return to Miami, Harry walked into their apartment, carrying two bulging envelopes containing photographs of their trip to Mexico.

'Oh, good,' Betty said, grabbing them from Harry. 'You couldn't have timed it better. I was just about to leave for my bridge club.'

'I thought you had already left,' he said, nervously. 'Why don't you go ahead and I'll check them over and toss out the ones that didn't come out.'

'Nonsense,' Betty replied as she spread the photographs on the dining room table. 'I want to take them with me to show them to the girls. Hey, they really came out good, didn't they?' She looked over the photographs with fondness. When she came to a picture of a young man and a woman sitting in a crowded arena, her mind went blank and she turned to Harry. 'I don't remember this one. Maybe the photo shop made a mistake.' She studied the photograph closer and it suddenly came to her. It was of the young man from the restaurant.

She shook her head. 'You sure had me

fooled, Harry. I really thought you had put it out of your mind. After thirty years, I guess I should have known better.'

'Look, I didn't want you to worry about me. It was something I had to do. The whole thing is as vivid to me now as it was forty-four years ago and his face . . . well, it's still there and like it or not it will be with me forever. Don't you see? I had to find out who he was, for my own peace of mind. But anyway, there's nothing to be concerned about. After what he told me, I'm convinced that — '

'You actually talked with him?'

'Yes, I talked with him. Now, I know what you're thinking, but there was really nothing to it. I didn't make a scene or anything like that. I talked with him at the restaurant, the day I went down to get us a couple of beers, remember? It wasn't easy for me, but I did it. Afterward, I felt a sense of relief to know that he couldn't possibly be the son of the SS officer.'

'Well, what's done is done,' she said.

Before Harry could object, she picked up the photograph, ripped it in half and threw it into a trash can. 'There's no sense keeping it in the house,' she said. 'Why risk holding on to something that might trigger unpleasant memories later on? I just want you to put the whole thing behind you.'

Harry nodded and smiled at her. 'You always seem to know what's best for me, Betty. If you hadn't thrown it away, I probably would've hidden it someplace in the apartment. And yes, I probably would've looked at it now and then and made myself miserable.'

★ ★ ★

Later, as Harry sat alone in the living room, he began to think about the photograph. It occurred to him that it was a good likeness of the SS officer from Poland. He wondered if it would do any good to show it to someone who might know his name. He got up, retrieved the torn pieces and carefully taped them together.

Holding the reassembled photograph in his hand, he tried to think of the people he knew who might be able to assist him. He considered calling his friend, Peter, a survivor of Auschwitz, but quickly dismissed the thought because he knew that Peter's mind had become too fragile. Then he remembered a letter he had received several months ago from Meyer Bergman of the Nazi Documentation Center in Amsterdam. It was a request for a donation and he had put the letter away with the idea that he would send them something later on, but he never got around to doing it. Quickly, he went to the closet in the bedroom and pulled out a large cardboard box full of old letters, many of which he'd been keeping for reasons he could no longer remember. He searched for the letter with Bergman's distinctive emblem and found it, along with a past due bill for some mail order shoes that he'd never received.

Eagerly he sat down to write a letter. He explained the circumstances surrounding his encounter with Antonio and requested assistance in putting a name to the face on the photograph.

*　*　*

Walking down the Paseo de la Reforma Antonio spotted Dr Pacheco as he was about to get into a cab. He waved and called out to him.

'*Hola*, Antonio,' responded Dr Pacheco, a tall, gray-mustached man in his late fifties.

Antonio hadn't seen him in a long time and he walked over to shake his hand. 'It's good to see you. How've you been?'

'Oh, you know me. I just try to get from one day to the next. And yourself?'

'Can't complain. My practice is beginning

to build up and I'm thinking of taking on a partner. It'll give me more time to do some of the things I keep putting off, like taking that trip to Italy that I've always talked about.'

'Good, I'm glad to hear things are going well for you. And your mother, how's she doing?'

'Well, as a matter of fact I'm a little worried. It's probably nothing, but a few days ago she suddenly had this dizzy spell. She thought it might be those pills you prescribed for her blood pressure.'

'Pills?' Dr Pacheco said with a puzzled look. 'I haven't prescribed any pills for her. In fact, the last time I saw her — three or four weeks ago — I commented to her about how well she had managed to keep her blood pressure down. There was no need to prescribe any medication for her, certainly not for her blood pressure.'

'Hmm, that's strange,' Antonio said. 'But you know mother. She can be very secretive at times. Well, more than likely, it was some over-the-counter pills she took.'

The taxi driver sounded his horn. 'Look, I've got to run,' Dr Pacheco said, his hand reaching to open the door. 'In a few days, if you're still worried about her, why don't you have her come to my office. She won't even have to make an appointment. Just call me, though, to make sure I'm in.'

'Thank you,' Antonio said. 'I'll talk to her about it.' He waved to him as the taxi drove away and disappeared into the early morning traffic.

Antonio continued down the Paseo de la Reforma and stopped at a news stand to pick up the morning paper. *'Hola, qué tal?'* he said to the old man behind the news stand. He was about to walk away when he glanced at a German magazine with the face of a Marlene Dietrich lookalike on its cover. 'I see you got some new magazines,' he said, pointing to it.

'That's not a new magazine,' the old man replied in a matter-of-fact way. 'I've been selling German magazines for years. Of course, not many people buy them, but I keep them in stock for the Germans who live in the neighborhood, mostly old people. As long as they ask for them, I'll always stock a few copies.'

'Funny thing,' Antonio said. 'I've been stopping here every morning for two years and I never noticed them before. Well, it just goes to show I'm not very observant.'

It dawned on him that as a result of his conversation with Friedman, he had become aware of anything German and it bothered him for reasons he couldn't explain. The incident with the magazine had not been the first. Just two days before, as he was turning the pages of the newspaper, he happened to spot a small notice tucked away on the corner of the page. It was an announcement for the local German club's bi-monthly meeting.

★   ★   ★

Five weeks had passed since Harry had sent the letter to the Nazi Documentation Center. Allowing for the slowness of the mail and the distance involved, he figured it would be at least another week before he received a response. That same morning, he went down to the lobby, as usual, to check his box. To his surprise, the letter he had been expecting had arrived. He tore open the envelope.

Dear Mr Friedman,
    We appreciate you sending us the information concerning the SS officer who caused you so much pain and suffering. With regard to the photograph you enclosed, my staff compared it to many of the photographs in our files and came up with an old, faded picture of a mid-level SS officer who looks like the man in your photograph. The man's name is Hans Schumann. He is believed to have

supervised the murder of at least 600 Jews during his brief assignment in Poland.

Our last report on him was dated 1955 when we received information that he had been spotted in Mexico City in the company of Alfred Schmidt, a member of the Aryan Knights of the Fatherland. Mexico is not considered a safe haven for them and he was probably in Mexico City for only a brief period of time.

As you may, or may not know, the Aryan Knights of the Fatherland is a secret international organization whose primary objective is to provide refuge and assistance to Nazi fugitives. It is headquartered in Buenos Aires and is made up mostly of expatriated Germans and ex-Nazis. The Aryan Knights of the Fatherland is a powerful organization which is prepared to protect the Nazis at all cost. For your safety, do not, I repeat, do not discuss this matter with anyone.

We are currently working on another fugitive and I don't know when I'll be able to assign someone to this case. Rest assured that we have every intention of following up your information, and as soon as we do, we will let you know.

Sincerely,
Meyer Bergman

'Nineteen fifty-five,' Harry whispered. If Schumann had fathered a baby while in Mexico, the baby would be thirty years old. He slipped the letter back in the envelope and walked to a pay phone at the end of the street. With the help of an operator, he placed a call to Antonio in Mexico City.

'My name is Harry Friedman from Miami, Florida,' he said to the secretary who answered. 'May I speak with Mister de la Vega?'

The secretary put Harry on hold while she spoke to Antonio over the intercom. 'There's a Mister Harry Friedman calling from Miami, Florida. Do you want to speak to him?'

For a moment Antonio couldn't recall the name. He instructed her to take a message.

'Wait, Maria,' he said, suddenly remembering. 'Let me speak to him.'

He cleared his throat before speaking. 'Hello, Mister Friedman, what can I do for you?'

'Forgive me for bothering you like this,' Friedman said. 'But I wanted to talk to you about . . . about something that may be of interest to you.'

'Yes, I'm listening.'

'Well, it's about a letter I received from the Nazi Documentation Center.'

'The Nazi Documentation Center?'

'It's an organization which is dedicated to hunting down ex-Nazis. They look for them all over the world.'

'What does that have to do with me?'

'Do you remember the photograph I took of you at the bull ring?'

'Yes, I remember.'

'Well, I sent it to the Nazi Documentation Center in Amsterdam. Not because it was a picture of you, but because it happened to look so much like the SS officer that I talked to you about. I must say that I was surprised at the information that came back to me. They actually identified the SS officer for me. His name is Hans Schumann.'

'That's all very interesting. But again, what does that have to do with me?'

'I just thought you would find it interesting to know that the last information received by the Nazi Documentation Center concerning Schumann was in 1955. He was seen in Mexico City in the company of a known member of the Aryan Knights of the Fatherland from Argentina.'

'Look,' Antonio said, a hostile edge to his voice, 'if you're trying to find out if it is possible this Schumann could be my father, you're wasting your time and mine. A few weeks ago I tried to answer your questions as best as I could, but I'm afraid this has gone too far and I'm really not interested in the letter you received because it has nothing to do with me. I told you once and I'll tell you again; I am not German and my father was not German. Now, if you'll excuse me, I'm extremely busy. Please do not bother me again.'

4

They were sitting in a corner booth towards the back of the crowded, noisy tavern located in the workers' section of Amsterdam. Both were German and both had the same expression of discomfort at having to be there. The older of the two, a tall, heavy-set man in his late sixties, kept looking at his watch.

'What's keeping him?' he said as he puffed on his cigarette.

'Relax, Walter,' said the other one, a thin, serious-faced man in his mid-sixties. 'He'll be here. Has he ever let us down before?'

'No, but that's only because we pay him very well for his information. That's something that really gets to me. He says he believes in what we stand for, but yet he's not willing to help us unless we pay him. In the old days, a man like that would not have been tolerated. As far as I'm concerned, he's worse than a Jew. And another thing, he's Swiss, not German. How can he possibly understand what we're trying to do? I say we get rid of the bastard the first chance we get.'

'I know how you feel, but we need him. We

were sent here to develop someone with access to the Nazi Documentation Center and that's what we've done. We have no choice but to put up with him, at least until we develop somebody else to take his place.'

'But Werner,' Walter said. 'I think that — ' He looked across the room and saw a slightly-built young man, with long, stringy, blond hair enter the tavern. 'There he is. He's half an hour late as usual.'

The young man spotted them and made his way to their booth. He seated himself next to Walter who turned to him and said, 'You're late, Bernard. For being Swiss, you're not very punctual are you?'

'Never mind about that,' Werner said. 'What do you have for us?'

The young man had a cocky look in his eye and waited a few seconds before answering. 'Before we talk about that, let's talk about something that's been bothering me for some time,' he said in a slow, deliberate manner. 'Both of you seem to forget that I'm the one who is taking all the risks. I realize that to you I'm just a simple mail carrier, but I'll tell you something. I'm smart enough to know that if the police should ever find out what we're doing, I'm the one who will go to jail. The two of you have it safe and easy, don't you? Well, I've been giving it a lot of thought and I think it's only fair that you increase my payments.'

Walter could hardly contain his anger. 'We're not going to give you a penny more than we usually do. We pay you too much as it is. We made a deal, remember? As I recall you said the money was not all that important and that you simply wanted to do your part to help the Aryan Knights.'

'Look, I don't care about what we agreed upon before,' Bernard snapped. 'Things are different now and I've got to look out for myself. The fact is, you need me more than I need you. It's as simple as that. I wasn't going to mention it, but I'm sure you're aware that Bergman would love to know what you're up to. He'd be willing to pay plenty for what I know. Of course, I would never consider going to him, unless you simply refuse to treat me the way I should be treated.'

'Perhaps you're right,' Werner said, condescendingly. 'You've become very important to us and we shouldn't be arguing over a few extra dollars, should we? If that's the only thing that's bothering you, I see no problem in augmenting your payments.'

Walter was about to protest but one look from Werner convinced him otherwise.

Werner continued. 'Now that we've settled

that, tell us what you have for us.'

'Very well,' Bernard said with a smug look on his face. 'I'll tell you what Bergman has been up to. I steamed open a few of his letters as I usually do and I found two letters that I think you'll be extremely interested to hear about.'

'Go on,' Walter said.

'The first letter was written by a Jew from America.' He paused to review his notes from a piece of paper. 'His name is Harry Friedman from Miami Beach, Florida. Friedman had apparently met a young man in Mexico City who looked like the SS officer that had killed his family in Poland. He enclosed a photograph of this young man and requested that Bergman attempt to identify the SS officer from the likeness in the photograph.'

'Very interesting,' Werner said, jotting Friedman's name on a three-by-five card. 'Did the letter mention the name of the young man?'

'Yes. His name is Antonio de la Vega. But that's not the good part. A few weeks later, Bergman sent Friedman a letter in which he said that the photograph of the young man matched the photograph of an SS officer named Hans Schumann who had last been spotted in Mexico City in 1955. He promised to assign someone to the case, but not right away.'

'What else did he say?' Walter asked.

Bernard looked at his notes. 'That's about it. He did warn him about the Aryan Knights, of course. What about this Hans Schumann? Have you heard of him? Is he being protected by the Aryan Knights?'

Walter and Werner looked at each other. They pretended not to recognize the name.

'Offhand, the name doesn't sound familiar,' Werner said. 'He's probably some low-level Nazi who may have requested help from the Aryan Knights at one time or another. We'll have to check with Buenos Aires to find out if they've heard of him. You did very well, Bernard.' He reached into his wallet and pulled out several bills which he folded in half. He glanced around the room to make sure no one was watching and gently placed the money under a napkin and moved it towards Bernard.

Bernard took the napkin and the money and placed it on his lap. He quickly counted the money. With a grin on his face, he looked up and said, 'That's more like it. As long as you understand that I'm worth the money you pay me, we'll have no problems. I'll call you when I develop more information.' He got up and slowly walked away.

Werner took a big gulp of beer and waited until Bernard was well out of earshot before saying what was on his mind. 'Walter, for once, I have to admit you were right. The son of a bitch has become a liability and we can't afford to take any chances with him.'

'If I were younger, I'd do it myself,' Walter said. 'Are we going to use Fritz?'

'Yes, get in touch with him as soon as possible.'

'What about the old Jew and the young man from Mexico?' Walter asked. 'And what about Schumann? When Bernard mentioned his name, I was really surprised. Buenos Aires is not going to be too happy about this.'

'Well, that's not our problem,' Werner said. 'We'll send the information to Buenos Aires and let them decide what they want to do about it. I'm sure they'll find a way of neutralizing the situation. They usually do.'

★ ★ ★

The living room was dimly lit, and the only sound that could be heard was coming from the television which was showing *Casablanca*. At one point, the familiar theme song swelled to such a level that neither Harry nor Betty could hear the doorbell ringing. The music subsided and the doorbell rang again. It was followed by a heavy knock.

'Who could that be at this time of night?' Betty asked, a hint of irritation in her voice.

'I'll see who it is,' Harry said. He got up and walked towards the door and opened it, just slightly.

It was Antonio. By the expression on his face, Harry could tell that Antonio had learned the truth about his father.

'I guess you know why I'm here,' Antonio said, barely audible. 'I have to talk to you.'

Harry paused for a moment, then stepped into the hallway. 'Look, I don't want my wife to know anything about this. Give me a second.' He stepped back inside the apartment, just long enough to tell Betty that it was the janitor wanting to show him the new security system.

They walked down the hallway and took the elevator to the main lobby. 'I know a coffee shop at the end of the street where we can talk,' Harry said.

'Okay,' Antonio said.

As they stepped into the warm, humid night, Harry said, 'You know, I kind of figured you'd get in touch with me. But I didn't think you'd show up on my doorstep.'

'Well, to tell you the truth I debated with myself for quite a while before coming here. But I didn't know where else to go. For the first time in my life, I feel as though . . . as though everything that I ever took for granted was a lie.' He shook his head.

'I know what you must be feeling,' Harry said. 'In a way I feel responsible. But when I saw you that day at the restaurant, well, I just had to see it through. I hope you understand.'

Antonio didn't say anything.

When they arrived at the coffee shop, Harry led the way to a corner table next to the window.

'Just bring us some coffee,' Harry said to the waitress who walked towards them.

They sat in silence until the waitress returned and placed the two cups of coffee on the table. 'Will there be anything else?' she asked.

'No, that'll be all,' Harry answered. He dropped a heaped teaspoon of sugar into his coffee and stirred it slowly. He waited for Antonio, who was staring out of the window, to say something.

Antonio finally turned to Harry, and he said, 'After your phone call, I knew that my worst fears had come true. I had been hoping that it was all just some kind of mistake and that in time this whole thing would be forgotten.' He paused. 'I confronted my mother. She told me everything. I still find it hard to believe . . . to accept what she said.

Since I talked with her last night, that's all I've been able to think about. Then I thought about you and I knew that you would be the one person who could understand how I felt.'

Friedman nodded, sympathetically. 'Did your mother confirm that your father's name was Hans Schumann?'

'She did. Actually she knew very little about him. She was introduced to him by a friend and I guess you could say it was love at first sight, at least it was for my mother. You have to understand, she was very young. Germans, Nazis, they meant nothing to her. Well, they saw each other for a few weeks, mostly secretly because her father would not have allowed her to go out unchaperoned. That's the way it was in those days. She fell deeply in love with him and she assumed that someday he would ask her to marry him. The rest is, well . . . just like a sad romance novel. One day he just left town and never came back.'

'Did he ever write to her after that?'

'No, she never heard from him again. Of course, she was devastated. But worse than that, she was pregnant. When I was born, she took the name de la Vega as her married name. De la Vega was an old boyfriend who had gotten killed in a plane crash. She created a clever background for him, one that could not easily be verified. She planned that when I became old enough to understand, she would tell me the truth. Of course, she never did, until now.'

'And your mother knew nothing about his past?'

'She knew very little about him. She knew he had fought in the war, but that's about it. He only revealed to her what he wanted her to know.'

Harry took a long sip of his coffee. 'I want you to know something,' he said. 'I know how hard it's been for you to talk about this and I appreciate that you came all this way just to see me. But . . . if your father were sitting here in this room I'd probably want to kill him. I can't apologize for the way I feel.'

'I don't blame you,' Antonio said. 'As a matter of fact, I feel as strongly as you do. That's why I've decided that I'm going to look for him. No matter how long it takes or how far I have to travel, I'm going to try to find him.'

'And if and when you find him, what then?'

There was a long silence. 'I don't know. But you can be sure that I won't stand in the way of his capture, if it comes to that.'

'I'm glad to hear that,' Harry said. 'If I can

38

help you in any way, I hope you'll let me know. I mean it. By the way, in the letter I received from the Nazi Documentation Center, the director, Meyer Bergman, promised to look into your father's case. They're working on something else right now and he didn't know how soon he could send someone out. They have your name, so there's a possibility that someone from the Center may try to contact you. Do you have any idea where you'll begin your search?'

'Well, I thought about going to Queretaro, just north of Mexico City. My mother told me that my father had mentioned a friend who lived there, a German by the name of Heinrich or Heimlich, she really wasn't sure. He had a jewelry store in the old part of town. That's all she knew about him. It's not much to go on, but it's as good a place as any to start.'

Harry looked at his watch. 'I've got to get back to the apartment before my wife begins to wonder what happened to me. Why don't you walk back with me? We can talk some more on the way.'

'You go ahead,' Antonio said. 'I just want to sit here for a while. I still have a few things to go over in my mind. I'm taking a late night flight back to Mexico City and I might as well wait here as in the airport.'

'Okay,' Harry said as he got up to leave. He pulled out a pen from his shirt pocket and wrote down his phone number on a paper napkin and handed it to Antonio. 'Call me when you find something. Good luck.'

5

The nude figures of a man lying on a bed with a woman sitting next to him and another woman sitting near his feet, were barely visible in the semi-darkened room of a Paris hotel. The only light came from a flickering candle which the woman sitting next to him used as a source of heat to warm the oil in a glass vial. Holding the candle with one hand and the vial with the other, she kept the flame underneath the vial until the oil was just the right temperature. She then placed the candle on the nightstand and turned to the nude, muscular body beside her to give him her undivided attention. With the skill of a woman accustomed to giving pleasure to men, she poured a small amount of oil over his chest and gently began to rub it into his skin. At the same time, the woman sitting near his feet gently massaged his toes and occasionally licked them with the tip of her tongue. She knew exactly how to produce the right sensations and slowly licked her way up the ankle and around the calf.

Suddenly the phone rang. The two women

stopped what they were doing and waited for Fritz to answer the phone.

'I told you to hold all my calls,' he said angrily.

'I'm sorry, sir, but the caller says it's important,' said the hotel operator. 'He told me to tell you that it's about your grandfather. He's very ill and not expected to live.'

Fritz understood the message. It was the coded signal that selected clients used whenever they wished to hire his services.

'Put him on,' he said.

'Sorry to disturb you,' said the voice on the other end. 'But I thought you should know that your grandfather is dying. He's not expected to live beyond the next forty-eight hours. The family thinks you should come home as soon as possible to see him while he's still alive. Can you make it?'

Fritz hesitated for a moment, then said, 'Tell the family I'll be there by noon tomorrow.' He hung up and looked at the two women.

'Where were we?' he said with a sly grin.

★ ★ ★

The walls of the library inside the 100-year-old mansion located on the outskirts of

Buenos Aires were covered with all sorts of German plaques, artifacts and war memorabilia ranging from the familiar swastika to actual battle-front photographs. Curiously absent was a large picture or painting of Hitler, though there were small, framed photographs of him in the company of well-known generals and admirers. The atmosphere in the room was unmistakably German, as was the nationality of the three elderly men who had convened that night to discuss the latest news from Amsterdam. They were seated around a coffee table cluttered with empty beer bottles and dirty ashtrays.

'We are all in agreement, then,' Alfred said as he stood up to adjourn the meeting. 'We will maintain a close watch on the old Jew and the young man from Mexico.'

Josef and Alexander voiced approval and offered no further comments. They stood up and prepared to follow Alfred out of the library.

The door of the room suddenly swung open and a young boy just barely old enough to talk excitedly made a beeline to where his grandfather was standing. Right behind him was the maid.

'Pablo, Pablo, come back here,' she said. She finally got hold of him. 'I'm sorry señor.

He got away from me when I wasn't looking.'

'That's all right,' Alfred said. 'Let him stay. We were just about to break up anyway.'

Pablo giggled with delight and reached for his grandfather's hand. '*Abuelo, vamos a jugar. Dónde está mi pelota.*'

Josef, the eldest of the three, shook his head. 'It has finally come to this. Our grandchildren speak only Spanish. Is our language and heritage to be totally forgotten?'

'He's right,' Alexander interjected. 'We have allowed ourselves to become absorbed by another culture, people as inferior as the Jews. When we first arrived here, we just wanted to hide. We settled for less than we should have. And now look at us . . . '

'You all seem to forget that we're lucky to be alive,' Alfred said. 'We came here in order to survive. And so, many of us married native women. What other choice did we have? We all knew we could never return to Germany.'

The exchange of emotion-filled comments continued as they slowly made their way out of the library. It was an especially sore topic, one that invariably produced bitter feelings about the way things had turned out for them. For Josef and Alexander, both former

Nazi officers who had ardently supported the idea of a Master Race, it seemed especially hard to accept the greatest irony of it all — that their children and grandchildren were anything but Aryan.

6

It was approaching 3 p.m. when Bernard showed up at the small, out-of-the-way restaurant, parked his bicycle in front and walked around to the rest-rooms at the rear of the building. Whistling a poor rendition of *Edelweiss* he entered the rest-room and went straight to the urinal where he unzipped his pants and proceeded to relieve himself. Holding his penis with his right hand, he looked down with child-like fascination at the way the amber stream splashed on to the walls of the urinal. He paid no attention to the sound of the door opening behind him. Suddenly he felt a muscular arm wrap tightly around his throat.

Bernard's strength was no match for Fritz's powerful grip, and all he could do was give a series of muted gasps that lasted almost sixty seconds, the time it took for his brain to be deprived of its essential oxygen. Fritz maintained the pressure for a few seconds longer to make sure he was dead. He released his hold and allowed Bernard's body to slump to the floor. His head came to rest just inside the base of the urinal where it covered the drain and caused the steady trickle of cleansing water to slowly spill on to the floor. Fritz took a few steps backwards and then calmly turned around and walked out of the rest-room.

★　★　★

Antonio had spent most of the day in Queretaro trying to find the jewelry store owned by his father's friend. Of the dozen or so people he spoke with, none recognized the name Heimlich or Heinrich, nor recalled any German ever having owned a jewelry store in the old part of town.

Sitting in an outdoor café, Antonio wondered if maybe his mother had been mistaken. Thirty years was a long time and there was more than a good chance that her recollection of names and events was a little unreliable. Maybe the jewelry store was outside of town, or maybe the man's name was not even close to what she remembered.

After paying the bill, he stood up and walked past a table where an elderly couple had just been seated. Their conversation was just loud enough for his ear to catch a few words of what sounded like German. He stopped and turned to them.

'Excuse me,' he said. 'I couldn't help but

overhear you talking. Are you German, by any chance?'

'Why, yes,' the gentleman replied, a puzzled look on his face.

'I'm sorry to interrupt like this. I'm an attorney from Mexico City and I came here looking for someone who used to live here many years ago. He's German and unfortunately I haven't had much luck finding anyone who has even heard of him. When I heard you speaking German, I thought that you might — '

'What's his name?'

'Heimlich or Heinrich . . . I'm not really sure. He used to own a jewelry store in the old part of town. But I'm afraid that was many years ago; thirty, in fact.'

'Do you know his first name or where he used to live?' the old man asked.

Antonio shook his head. 'I don't even know if he's still alive. You see, I need to find him to . . . to take a deposition from him. It concerns a transaction between him and my client. Heinrich, or whatever his name is, sold my client what he thought were ordinary art objects many years ago. Recently they were discovered to be quite valuable and my client now has the problem of proving they are legally his. At the time, the deal was sealed with a handshake, which I'm afraid is not legally binding. So, unless I locate this gentleman, my client will be involved in a legal dispute for years to come.'

'I see,' the old man said. 'And you're sure his name was Heimlich or Heinrich?'

'No, not really,' Antonio replied. 'It could've been something different, perhaps something that sounded like that.'

'Wait a minute,' he said, turning to his wife. 'Could it be the man who used to live across from the cathedral? He used to own a shop. Come to think of it, it was a jewelry shop.'

His wife nodded. 'Yes, I remember. If he's the one I'm thinking of, he used to be married to a Mexican woman. They had a beautiful little girl as I recall.'

'Of course,' the old man said, turning back to Antonio. 'It must be him. But his name was Heydrich, not Heimlich or whatever you said. You're right, it was a long time ago. He lived in Queretaro for several years. Didn't much like it here. That's why he moved to Guadalajara. But you won't find him there, though. About seven or eight years ago I ran into him at the airport in Mexico City. Actually, it was he who recognized me as I was waiting for a flight to Germany. If he hadn't spoken to me, I probably wouldn't have recognized him. He had lost a lot of weight and his hair was almost all white. His wife had died the year before. He was catching a flight to El Paso where he planned to live with his daughter and her family.'

'Did he happen to mention what his daughter's married name was or anything else that may help me find where she lives?'

'As a matter of fact, he wrote down his daughter's name and address on a piece of paper and he gave it to me. He told me to look him up if I ever visited El Paso. I kept the piece of paper for a long time afterwards, but then I think I threw it away or something. It was so long ago, it's hard to remember.'

Antonio stepped closer. 'It's really important to me. Can you try to remember what he wrote on the paper? Her husband's name, her address, anything at all?'

The old man thought about it. 'I'm not really sure, but I think the daughter's married name was Sanchez . . . Santos. Something like that. I just can't remember, but I'm pretty sure it started with San. As for the address, my mind is a blank. There is one thing though that may be of help to you. He told me that his son-in-law worked as a maintenance man at some museum. The Museum of Art, I believe.'

Smiling, Antonio left the restaurant and took a cab to the train station.

★ ★ ★

'To Reforma and Versalles,' Antonio said, getting into a cab in front of the train station in Mexico City.

A few minutes later, the taxi deposited him in front of his apartment building. He was greeted by the doorman who told him he had a visitor waiting for him in the lobby.

'He got here about an hour ago,' the doorman said. 'I suggested he leave his name and phone number. But he said he preferred to wait, so I told him he could wait in the lobby.'

'*Gracias*, Manuel.'

Antonio entered the lobby and approached the visitor sitting in a large peacock chair facing the entrance. The man had a large, tanned face with a wide nose and a full head of tousled brown hair. He was wearing a light linen coat that fitted snugly over his tall, beefy frame. 'Señor de la Vega?' he said as he stood up and extended his hand.

'Yes. The doorman said you've been waiting for me for quite a while. If it's about a case you want me to handle for you, I'm afraid I won't be able to help you. I'm not taking any new cases and — '

'Forgive me for interrupting, but I didn't come here to hire you as my lawyer. My name

51

is Jacob Linsky. I'm with the Nazi Documentation Center in Amsterdam. I'd like to talk to you about a rather important matter that recently came to our attention.'

'You're here to find out about my ... about Hans Schumann, aren't you?' Antonio said, recalling his conversation with Friedman.

The man gave a nervous glance at the stream of people walking in and out of the building. 'Look, is there somewhere we can talk? That is, if you don't mind.'

'I know a place just down the street,' Antonio said. 'At this hour, it shouldn't be too crowded.' They stepped out of the building and walked the short distance to a bar located off to one side of a small hotel. They entered the bar and took a table against the wall towards the back.

A waiter came up and took their order, dry vermouth on the rocks for Antonio and gin and soda for Linsky. While they waited for their drinks, they talked about Friedman and his letter to Meyer Bergman.

'I must say, I'm really surprised at the way you're taking all of this,' Linsky said. 'Before coming here, I worried about how you would receive me. I mean, there's little doubt that Schumann is your father and the thought ran through my mind that you might want to protect him.'

Antonio became suddenly defensive. 'Look, until a few days ago I had never even heard of Schumann. I can assure you that I have no positive feelings for him and the last thing I would want to do is protect him.'

'I'm glad to hear that,' Linsky said. 'That will make my work a whole lot simpler. You just don't know how many times I've had doors slammed in my face the moment I start to ask a few questions about a Nazi fugitive. But enough of that, the main reason — '

He paused to allow the waiter to deliver their drinks. 'As I was saying, the main reason I'm here is to try to come up with some good leads that will help us locate Schumann.'

'I understand,' Antonio said, nodding. 'I'll help you any way I can. As a matter of fact, I had already decided to look for him myself.'

'Really,' Linsky said, taking a sip of his drink.

'Yes, the day I confronted my mother I learned that my father used to visit a friend of his, a German who lived in Queretaro, just north of here. I had just arrived from there when I met you at the lobby.'

'Did you find him?'

'No, I didn't. He hadn't lived there in years. A German couple who knew him — Heydrich was his name — told me he was

53

living in El Paso just across the border from Ciudad Juarez. He went there to live with his daughter and her family after his wife died. They couldn't give me an address or anything else, except that his son-in-law is supposed to be working as a maintenance man at the Museum of Art. Unfortunately, they couldn't remember his name. I was planning on taking the first flight to El Paso tomorrow morning to see what I could find.'

'Since you're obviously serious about finding your father, why don't we work together?' Linsky said. 'Between us we're bound to come up with some good leads.'

'That's fine with me. What did you have in mind? Do you want to accompany me to El Paso?'

'I would like to,' Linsky answered. 'But I think we can cover more ground if you go ahead as planned while I stay here in Mexico City. There are a few people, friends of the Nazi Documentation Center, that I want to contact to see if they know anything about him. When you get back we can compare notes and go on from there.'

'Good idea,' Antonio said. 'It shouldn't take me more than a couple of days. Where can I reach you when I return?'

'I'm staying at the El Presidente hotel. Call me the moment you get back. Oh, one last thing. Bergman would prefer to keep my mission a secret, so don't tell anyone — and that includes Friedman — that I'm here or what we plan to do. It's not that we don't trust him, it's just that the less he or anyone knows about our activities, the better.'

Antonio hesitated. 'Well, if that's the way you want it. But I don't think telling him anything is going to jeopardize your activities.'

'Trust me, I know what I'm talking about.' He leaned closer. 'We have to be extremely careful that the Aryan Knights — I'm sure you've heard of them — do not get wind of what we're up to. They seem to have eyes and ears everywhere, even in Miami.'

7

From the airport Antonio made a last-minute call to Friedman in Miami. There was no answer. He tried again five minutes later and Friedman answered on the second ring.

'I'm glad I caught you,' Antonio said, relieved to hear his voice. 'Thought I'd call to let you know what's happening. I'm at the airport, waiting for my flight to Ciudad Juarez.'

'What's in Ciudad Juarez?'

'It's across from El Paso. Remember that I planned on going to Queretaro to look for my father's friend? Well, I didn't find him, but I did run into an elderly German couple who used to know him. They said that after his wife died, he decided to move to El Paso to live with his daughter and her husband. It's not much to go on, but maybe I'll get lucky.'

'Well, like I said when you came to see me, if I can help you in any way, just let me know.'

'Thanks. I'll keep it in mind. Incidentally, a man named Jacob Linsky from the Nazi Documentation Center came to see me yesterday. He was waiting for me when I returned to my apartment from Queretaro. I

56

was really surprised to see him. Anyway, I told him about my trip to Queretaro and we agreed that it would be a good idea if we joined forces to try to locate my father.'

'That's good news,' Friedman said. 'I'm glad to know that my letter to Bergman did some good. With his organization behind you, there's no way you can fail.'

'There's one thing, though, that kind of bothered me,' Antonio said, hesitantly. 'After we finished talking, he told me he would prefer that I not tell you anything about what we planned to do. Naturally, I was surprised to hear him say that since it was you who had notified Bergman in the first place. He said it wasn't that he didn't trust you, but that Bergman wanted to keep his mission a secret. He seemed like a nice enough fellow, but afterwards I had to question his request not to talk to you. I'm sure there's nothing to it, but I thought you'd want to know.'

'Yes, I'm glad you told me,' Friedman replied, a trace of concern in his voice. 'I hope you'll continue to give me a call from time to time to let me know what's happening.'

An overhead speaker suddenly blared out a boarding call for the flight to Ciudad Juarez.

'Look, I've got to go now. I'll be staying at

the Embassy Towers in El Paso if you need to reach me. Wish me luck.'

★　★　★

At the car rental desk in Juarez, Antonio did not notice a tall man with a bushy mustache and long, wavy hair, standing on the other side of the terminal. Occasionally, the man would give a quick glance in Antonio's direction.

After a short time, Antonio walked out of the terminal, crossed the street to a parking lot and got into a black, two-door compact with a bent antenna and a hairline crack on the windshield.

The tall man waited a few seconds, then hurriedly walked towards his own car, a light blue sedan parked in the same lot. Seconds later, the compact slowly approached the exit gate, stopped briefly and made a left turn on to a road that led away from the airport. At the same time, the tall man cranked up his engine and cautiously pulled out behind the black compact. He followed from a safe distance all the way to the border, across the Rio Grande, and finally to the Embassy Towers Hotel in the eastern part of El Paso.

After checking in, Antonio went up to his

room and began to unpack. He spotted a phone book on top of the night stand and flipped through the pages beginning with the letters SAN. He shook his head. The list of possible names seemed endless. If only the German couple had remembered his name. He still had the Museum of Art to check out and he looked up the address and wrote it down on a piece of paper.

★ ★ ★

Sitting at his desk going over some bills, Friedman couldn't get out of his mind what Antonio had said about Linsky. It just didn't make sense that the Nazi Documentation Center would want to withhold information from him. He found the letter from Bergman and read it over again. It was a sincere letter and left him convinced that Bergman had no intention of keeping him in the dark.

Impulsively, he picked up the phone and placed a call to Bergman in Amsterdam.

A young woman answered. 'I'm sorry, but Mister Bergman is out of town,' she said. 'He's not expected to return until tomorrow morning.'

'But this is extremely important,' Friedman said. 'Surely you must have some way of getting in touch with him.'

'He usually calls in for messages. Would you care to leave one?'

Friedman hesitated, then gave her his name and phone number. 'I must talk to him as soon as possible. Do you understand? Tell him . . . just have him call me.'

★   ★   ★

The elevator doors opened and Antonio and two other guests got off on the lobby floor. A group of students was waiting to go up and he walked around them and made his way through the lobby, towards the exit door.

By the time he got to his car, the tall man had already spotted him and was ready to pull out behind him.

Antonio proceeded slowly out of the parking lot and headed north to pick up Montana Avenue.

Traffic was light and he arrived at the museum twenty minutes later.

The tall man parked his car a safe distance away.

As Antonio entered the building, he saw a young woman sitting behind the information desk.

'I'm trying to locate someone who works

here,' Antonio said. 'But unfortunately I don't know his name.' He repeated the story he'd used with the German couple in Queretaro. 'All I know is that his last name starts with San.'

'I've been working here for almost three years and I can't think of anyone with a name like that. Could it be something else?'

'I don't think so,' he said, disappointed. 'Is there any way of finding out if he used to work here? I mean, if it isn't too much trouble.'

She thought about it, then said, 'Let me check something.' She got up, walked over to a filing cabinet and returned with a thick manila folder.

Quickly, she flipped through some papers and paused when she spotted an old roster. 'We may be in luck,' she said with a quick smile. 'Could it be David Santiago? It's the only name that begins with San.'

'Santiago,' Antonio repeated. 'Yes, it could be the one. Do you have a phone number or an address?'

She shook her head. 'I'm sorry. It's just an ordinary roster. Evidently he must not have worked here very long, otherwise there would be more information on him.'

'Well, at least I have a name,' Antonio said. 'It's more than I had before.'

He was about to walk away when the woman said, 'You may want to check with Howard. He's our maintenance man. He's been working here a lot longer than I have. That's him over there by the water cooler.' She called out to him.

Howard finished taking a drink and tossed the paper cup into a can.

'Howard,' she said. 'This gentleman is trying to locate someone who used to work here a long time ago. His name is David Santiago. Do you remember him by any chance?'

'David Santiago . . . yes, I do remember him,' he said after a long pause. 'It's been about six, seven years. As I recall, he had a drinking problem. That's why he didn't last long.'

'It's very important,' Antonio said. 'Do you remember where he lived or anything else that might help me find him?'

'He kept to himself a lot and I never got to know him,' Howard said, starting to shake his head. 'On second thoughts, I do remember something. One time he asked me for a ride home and I seem to recall that I dropped him off at a house on Altura Street, not too far from here. I don't remember the address or what the house looked like, but you shouldn't have any trouble finding it.'

'Oh, why is that?' Antonio asked mildly surprised.

'There's a big statue of the Virgin of Guadalupe in the middle of his front lawn. You can't miss it.'

8

Still at his desk, Friedman heard the phone ring and he rushed to answer it. It was a wrong number.

He hung up the phone and seconds later it rang again. It was the same caller.

'You're dialling the wrong number,' he said, gruffly. 'Don't call here again.' He slammed down the phone and turned to walk away just as it rang yet again.

'Look young lady,' he shouted into the receiver. 'If you don't stop calling this number — '

'Excuse me?' the caller said. 'My name is Meyer Bergman and I would like to — '

'Mister Bergman, please forgive my rudeness. I thought you were someone else. The reason I called was about your recent letter concerning Hans Schumann. Perhaps you can clarify something for me.'

'Like I said in the letter we're very busy on other cases and I don't know when we'll be able to follow up on the information you gave us.'

'Then you didn't send anyone to Mexico to look for Schumann?'

'Of course not. We simply do not have the resources to go after every Nazi that people tell us about.'

Friedman gripped the phone tightly. 'Well, then something is very wrong.'

'What are you talking about?'

'A lot has happened since I got your letter. I've since found out that Antonio de la Vega is, in fact, the son of Hans Schumann. It's difficult to explain but we trust each other and I wouldn't want anything to happen to him. Anyway, Antonio called me from Mexico a few hours ago and told me that a person claiming to have been sent by you had met with him and offered to help him. The odd thing was that the man requested that he not tell me anything about it.'

'Mister Friedman, listen to me. Your friend is in danger. There is no question that the Aryan Knights are behind this. I don't know how they were able to find out about you or Antonio, but you must warn him as soon as possible. These people will stop at nothing, not even murder.'

Friedman could feel his chest begin to tighten. 'Yes, I understand,' he said, anxious to get off the phone. 'Thank you, Mister Bergman. I'll let you know what happens.'

Friedman pushed the disconnect button and dialled the number to Antonio's hotel in

El Paso. He waited impatiently as the operator connected him to Antonio's extension and let it ring six times. There was no answer. Frustrated, he hung up the phone and walked back to his desk. As he reached for a pencil, he felt a sharp pain in his chest and automatically placed his left hand over his heart. He was used to feeling the occasional pain and dismissed it as nothing to be alarmed about.

★　★　★

Back in his car, Antonio pulled out a map from the glove compartment and spread it across the steering wheel. Howard was right, he thought, putting his finger on Altura Street. It was just a few miles away. He put the map to one side, turned the ignition key and slowly pulled into Montana Avenue and headed back the way he had come.

The tall man watched him and waited for Antonio to get a safe distance ahead before pulling out.

Antonio continued east until he spotted a sign that said Altura St. He turned right and drove slowly down the street. The shrine was nowhere in sight. 'You can't miss it,' he mumbled. He pulled over to the kerb.

Maybe the guy moved and took the shrine

with him. He got out of the car, walked up to the nearest house and rang the bell. A few seconds later a young woman holding a baby opened the door.

'I'm sorry to bother you,' Antonio said. 'I'm trying to locate someone who's supposed to live on this street. Unfortunately, I don't have his address. Can you tell me — '

'We just bought this house a few months ago. Except for Missus Simpson, who lives next door, we don't know anyone on the street.'

'The man I'm looking for is supposed to have a religious shrine in the middle of his front lawn. Unless the statue is very, very small and I just couldn't spot it.'

'Oh, I think I know who you're talking about,' the young woman said. 'I remember Missus Simpson talking about him one time, shortly after we moved here. It seems that several people on the block objected to the shrine. It was almost five feet tall. Somehow, they were able to persuade him to remove it.' She stepped out on to the porch and pointed across the street. 'That's the one. Two houses down. The one with the yellow trim.'

'Thank you,' Antonio said, with a quick smile. He gave a playful tug on the baby's hand, then walked across the street toward the house with the yellow trim.

The tall man kept a watchful eye from inside his car parked at the end of the street.

Antonio approached the door and rang the bell. There was no answer. He went around the side of the house and saw a converted garage apartment set back toward the rear of the yard. It had a side door next to which a small rose bush was beginning to take hold. He walked up and knocked. A moment later he heard the sound of shuffling feet, then the door opened slowly to reveal a sombre-looking old man.

'If you're looking for David, he's out of town,' the old man said before Antonio had a chance to say anything. 'Won't be back for several days.'

The accent was definitely German.

'Well, actually I wanted to speak with you,' Antonio said.

'With me?' the old man said, mildly surprised.

'You are Mister Heydrich, aren't you?'

'I am Wolfgang Heydrich. What do you want?'

'May I come in? I will explain everything.'

The old man hesitated, then opened the door wider.

'Come inside,' he said. 'You'll have to forgive the mess. I live alone and I'm not much of a housekeeper. My wife, God rest

her soul, always picked up after me. But now
. . . here, sit down on this chair. But wait just
one moment while I get my glasses. My
eyesight has got worse the past few years and
it bothers me to carry on a conversation with
people when I can't see what they look like.
What a curse it is to get old.' He walked over
to an antique nightstand and picked up a pair
of wire-rimmed glasses. 'That's much better,'
he said as he put them on.

He turned to look at Antonio and his eyes
suddenly widened. 'Forgive me for staring,'
he said, taking a seat across from him. 'It's
unbelievable, but you look like . . . like
someone I used to know.'

'Like Hans Schumann?' Antonio said.

The old man seemed uncertain whether or
not to acknowledge the name. 'Who are you,
anyway?' he asked suspiciously. 'How did you
get my name?'

'Permit me to explain. My name is Antonio
de la Vega. I live in Mexico City and I
recently discovered that . . . that your friend
Hans Schumann is my father. I know what
you're thinking, but please understand that
I'm not here to make trouble for anyone. All I
want to do is find him. You can understand
that, can't you?'

The old man hesitated. 'Why are you so
certain that he is your father, and why do you

69

think I can help you? I haven't seen him in — ' He stopped himself.

'So, he *was* your friend,' Antonio said.

'Well . . . yes, he was my friend,' the old man admitted.

'I was hoping you might help me find him,' Antonio said, trying to gain his sympathy. 'My mother wasn't much help, I'm afraid. But I really can't blame her. She told me what little she could about him. She was very young when she fell in love with him and . . . well, as you know things were different back then. Unfortunately she lost track of him but she was able to tell me that he used to visit you in Queretaro. She didn't tell me much more than that.'

Heydrich became noticeably uncomfortable. 'I haven't seen him in many, many years,' he said. 'In fact, the last time I saw him was about twenty-nine . . . thirty years ago, maybe longer. You see — ' He was interrupted by the ring of the telephone. 'Excuse me,' he said as he picked up the phone. 'Hello.' Brief pause. 'Oh, it's you, Missus Hansen. I'm afraid I have company at the moment. Can I call you back in a few minutes?'

While he waited for Heydrich to finish his conversation, Antonio stood up and looked around the clutter-filled room. There were

70

framed photographs of Heydrich and his family almost everywhere. All but a few were of the years spent in Mexico. As he stood in front of a round, English tea table, his eyes suddenly became fixed on a small, framed photograph of Heydrich and another person. They were standing in front of a hotel with the name Posada Del Sol just barely visible in the background. He picked up the photograph and looked at it closely. He could hardly believe it, the other person was his father. It was like seeing a photograph of himself.

Heydrich glanced nervously at Antonio. 'I told you I was busy, Missus Hansen,' he said, brusquely. 'I'll call you back later.'

Antonio returned the photograph to its place.

'It was taken just outside the hotel where your father had spent the night,' Heydrich said. 'I think I saw your father one time after that, maybe two or three months later. Yes, I'm positive that I saw him only once after that photograph was taken, twenty-nine . . . thirty years ago. My wife and I never heard from him after that. We just assumed that he had left the country for one reason or another.'

Antonio asked if there was anyone else who knew Schumann or who might have remained in contact with him throughout the years. 'Surely, he didn't just vanish without a trace.'

'I can understand your frustration and disappointment, young man, but I really don't know what else I can tell you. He may have had other friends but I did not know them, nor did he speak of any. We were just two Germans in a foreign land and that is mostly what we had in common. I'm sorry I could not be of more help to you.'

'Well, it looks like I've hit a dead end,' Antonio said, making his way towards the door. 'I had hoped you could provide me with something . . . anything.'

Heydrich opened the door to see him out and apologized again for not being able to help him. 'Good luck,' he said to him.

Walking back to his car, Antonio couldn't shake off the feeling that he had missed something during his brief conversation with Heydrich. Maybe it was because Heydrich had been so positive that he hadn't seen his father in almost thirty years.

★　★　★

'That's it!' Antonio said, suddenly braking and turning the car around. Heydrich had lied to him. The hotel in the photograph had changed its name. It all came back to him. He

72

and a group of students had been scheduled to stay at the same hotel. When they got there, they found it had closed for renovations. Shortly afterwards, the hotel changed its name from El Centro to Posada Del Sol. But that was at least seventeen years ago, which meant the photograph was taken about the same time or sooner. Heydrich had obviously tried his best to protect his father. But why? Was he a collaborator with the Aryan Knights? One way or another, he was going to get some straight answers from him.

Antonio sped all the way and arrived at the house a few minutes later. He parked in the driveway, got out and walked briskly to Heydrich's house. He was about to knock on the door when he noticed it was slightly ajar.

'Mister Heydrich. Mister Heydrich,' he called out to him. 'I need to speak to you.'

There was no answer.

Antonio slowly pushed the door open and walked into the house. He saw a floor lamp turned over and said, 'Mister Heydrich, are you all right?' He looked around and saw pieces of a broken ornament scattered next to the sofa. Cautiously, he took a few steps towards the closed door to the bathroom and reached to open it slowly. 'Oh, my God!' he gasped as he saw Heydrich's body sprawled across the floor, his hand clutching an extension cord that had been wrapped tightly around his neck.

For a second, Antonio remained frozen. The thought that somebody might have followed him to Heydrich's apartment frightened him. He reeled out of the bathroom, took a deep breath, then quickly began to rummage around the room.

He pulled out the small, overstuffed drawer of a rolltop desk, and a bunch of letters fell out. One of them, postmarked Asunción, Paraguay, caught his eye and he quickly opened it and flipped to the closing.

Written in a bold, European style, it said:

Your Friend,
Hans

He shoved the letter into his pocket, gave a final glance over the entire room and walked towards the door. On impulse, he grabbed the photograph of Heydrich and his father from the English tea table, and continued out of the apartment.

Moments later, he was on Montana Avenue travelling east.

★　★　★

Friedman picked up the phone and tried again to reach Antonio in El Paso. He allowed the phone to ring continuously. Bergman's comments about the Aryan Knights were difficult to ignore, and he worried more about Antonio's safety than he did about the pain in his chest which had gradually become more intense.

★ ★ ★

Entering his hotel, Antonio bypassed a small crowd waiting for the elevator and walked up three flights of stairs to get to his room. He could hear the phone ringing as he reached to insert the key in the door. Quickly, he stepped into the room and made a dash for the phone sitting on the night stand. In his haste, he allowed the door, with the key still in the lock, to swing shut behind him.

'Hello?' he answered, slightly out of breath. It was too late. The phone had stopped ringing.

Friedman had hung up and slumped to the floor, dead from a heart attack.

Antonio returned the receiver to its cradle and wondered who it could have been.

Without warning, the tall man suddenly stepped from behind and struck Antonio with a hard chop to the side of his neck, leaving him momentarily dazed. He struggled helplessly as the man grabbed the receiver and began to wrap its cord around Antonio's neck. Barely able to remain conscious, Antonio fell to his knees and tried frantically to free himself. But it was no use. The more Antonio struggled, the more the man tightened the cord.

At the same time, a maid pushing her cart down the hallway spotted the key in the door. She pulled her cart over and knocked on the door, then turned the key and let herself in. She let out a loud scream as she saw the two men struggling on the floor. Startled, the man turned to look at the maid and momentarily loosened his grip on the cord. It was just the break that Antonio needed and he pushed the man away, causing him to fall backwards.

Breathless and still on his knees, Antonio grabbed the receiver and quickly removed the cord from around his neck. He barely had a chance to regain his senses when the man suddenly scrambled to his feet and lunged directly at him. Instinctively, Antonio raised the receiver above his head and with all the strength he could muster, struck the assailant on the side of the head. The maid watched in horror and screamed even louder.

'Oh, my God, you killed him,' she said as she saw the man slump to one side. She ran out into the hallway, screaming and calling out for help.

The blow to the man's head had partially dislodged a thick hairpiece. Curious, but still shaken, Antonio moved closer. He noticed the left side of the man's bushy mustache was crooked and he reached over and pulled it right off. It was Jacob Linsky, the man he had met in Mexico City.

When the cops arrived, he gave them a statement and managed to convince them that it was a case of self defence. The maid backed him up and hours later he was finally allowed to leave.

* * *

At the local airport, the ticket agent stamped Antonio's boarding pass and dropped it into a folder. 'You're all set,' he said, handing him a ticket to Dallas. 'They're beginning to board. Better hurry.'

When he got to the departure gate he had just enough time to call Friedman to let him know what had happened. He saw an available phone and he walked towards it, a second too late.

'Sorry, but I'm in a hurry,' said a tall, well-dressed woman who stepped in front of him and reached for the phone. Antonio clenched his teeth and backed away slowly. His call to Friedman would have to wait.

★ ★ ★

The plane arrived in Dallas ahead of time and he wasted no time filing out of the plane to get to the nearest phone. He spotted one just ahead, and he stepped up and quickly dialled Friedman's number.

Seconds later, a young woman answered.

'May I speak to Mister Friedman?' Antonio asked, not sure he had dialled the right number.

There was a moment of silence, then the young woman said in a soft, trembling voice, 'May I ask who you are? Are you a friend of his?'

'My name is Antonio de la Vega and yes, I'm a friend of his. But why — '

'My father passed away,' she said. 'We think it was a heart attack. It happened a few hours ago and we're still very much in shock as you can imagine.'

Antonio was stunned. 'But how . . . I mean, I just talked with him early this morning and he sounded just fine. I don't know what to say. I'm sorry. I'm truly sorry.'

'Thank you.'

'I want you to know that although I didn't

know your father very well, I had a great deal of respect for him. He never mentioned that he had a daughter and I assumed it was just him and his wife.'

'Well, if you'll excuse me, Mister de la Vega, I have to make a lot of phone calls,' she said, trying to be polite.

'Of course, I understand. I just wish there was something I could do. Unfortunately, I'm . . . I'm on my way to Paraguay to take care of some business and I don't know if I'll ever have the chance to pay my respects in person.'

'Thank you again,' she said, barely able to contain her emotions. 'I'm sure my father valued your friendship. Goodbye.'

Antonio hung up the phone and stood there for a long time. Somehow the idea of going on to Paraguay didn't seem as important any more and he had to force himself to walk away to make his next connection.

9

Asuncion

'Your room is at the end of the hall, Señor de la Vega,' said the smiling, young woman from behind the front desk. She handed him a key with a long brass handle.

'By the way, maybe you can help me with something,' Antonio said. He pulled out Schumann's letter and read the address to her. 'Can you tell me if it is nearby?'

At the other end of the counter another hotel employee, a distinguished-looking man in his mid-fifties, suddenly cocked his head.

'It's about five blocks from here, just behind the Post Office,' she said. 'You shouldn't have any trouble finding it.'

'Thanks,' Antonio said as he walked away.

The distinguished-looking man looked up and waited until Antonio was well out of sight before stepping to one side to review his registration card. He made a mental note of the name and quickly walked into an adjoining office to make a call.

'Herman, it's Peter. I thought you might want to know that someone was just inquiring about Schumann's house. He had his exact address and wanted to know how to get there.'

'Who is he?'

'He registered under the name Antonio de la Vega from Mexico City,' Peter replied. 'I don't know anything else but I'll keep my eye on him.'

'Make sure that you do and call me immediately if he leaves the hotel. I'll talk to you later.'

★ ★ ★

His hand still clutching the phone, Herman placed a call to Buenos Aires.

'Let me speak to Alfred,' he said to the maid who answered the phone. 'Tell him it's Herman.'

'*Un momento*,' she said.

Alfred picked up the call in the study.

'Hello, Herman. How are things going?'

'Peter at the Chaco Hotel just called me and said that Antonio de la Vega had just registered at the hotel.'

'What!' Alfred said. 'Something must've gone wrong in El Paso. Perhaps we underestimated this young man from Mexico. Listen to me. I'm taking the next flight to Asunción. Meanwhile, get everyone together and make sure that Antonio does not leave the hotel. Is that understood?'

'I understand,' Herman replied. 'I'll post somebody in the lobby throughout the night.'

* * *

The next day Peter kept a watchful eye on the elevator and studied the face of each person that stepped off it. It was getting later and later and Antonio had still not come down. Suddenly the phone rang. It was Herman.

'Yes, he's still in his room,' Peter said. 'I've taken care of everything, just as you instructed.'

'Good,' Herman said. 'Call me the minute he leaves the hotel.'

Peter was about to hang up. 'Wait, Herman. He just came out of the elevator. I'll talk to you later.' Quickly, he stepped from behind the counter and followed Antonio to the exit door. He stopped just outside the doorway and signalled to the driver of a taxi cab parked off to one side of the driveway.

The driver acknowledged the signal and slowly drove up to where Antonio was standing. 'Taxi?' he asked.

'Yes,' Antonio said, getting into the back of the cab. 'I want to go to four eleven Alhambra Street.'

'Sí señor,' the driver responded as he stepped on the accelerator and slowly drove away. When he was about four blocks from the hotel, he made an abrupt turn into a narrow alley where two men brandishing hand guns suddenly forced themselves into the back seat.

'Don't try to resist,' one of the men said, jabbing a pistol into Antonio's chest.

'What's going on?' Antonio said, his wide eyes moving between the two men. 'What do you want from me?'

'You'll know soon enough,' the other man said. 'Just do like we say and keep quiet until we get where we're going.'

★ ★ ★

A half hour later, the cab pulled into a fortress-like compound where it parked in the rear, behind a three-storey mansion that had a door with a 'DO NOT ENTER' sign posted over the frame. The two men ordered Antonio out of the cab, then escorted him through an open doorway, down a steep, narrow stairwell that led to a large, dungeon-like room. A faint yet unmistakable odor of empty wine barrels, long-since removed, was the only evidence that the room had at one time been the family wine cellar. There were old and new implements of torture placed in a manner that made the room appear to be part of a museum of horror. One complete wall was covered with rusty-looking manacles and chains of all sizes and shapes. In the center was an exact replica of a French guillotine complete with a kneeling wax figure of Marie Antoinette waiting for the blade to detach her head from her body.

'You must forgive the way we brought you here,' said Alfred, a tall, square-faced man in his late sixties. He was standing to one side of the guillotine. 'But we weren't sure you would accept our invitation.' He paused to allow Antonio to look around, then added, 'Interesting room, isn't it? Our host is an avid collector of such things. Personally I find it — '

'Why have you brought me here?'

'Remarkable, absolutely remarkable,' said Herman, a short, stocky man in his early seventies. 'You're the very image of your father when he was young.'

'Come, let's sit down and be more comfortable,' Alfred said. He walked to an informal seating area in the corner of the room. 'We have much to talk about and we would like for it to be as pleasant as possible. The choice is up to you.'

Antonio followed and took a seat directly

across from them. 'Look, I don't know what this is all about,' he said. 'But if you think you can scare me into leaving town without seeing my father, it's not going to work. I've come a long way and I'm not going to give up that easily.'

'I admire your spunk, but for now, all we want you to do is listen to what we have to say,' Alfred said. 'First of all, I don't know how much you know about Germany and the role it played during the war, but I'm sure no one has told you the real truth. The fact is, we were doing the dirty work that no other country had the guts to do. Don't think for a moment that the so-called atrocities attributed to the Nazis were not committed without at least the tacit approval of many other countries.'

'That's right,' Herman added. 'The Nazis had the courage to take a stand for what they believed to be a noble idea. And don't forget, at the time, they were the only ones willing to act and speak out against the Communists.'

'What we're trying to say,' Alfred said, 'is that you shouldn't be so hasty in judging your father. He was after all, a soldier who was taught to obey orders. What right does anyone have after all these years to say that he and other Nazis were wrong in following orders set by the High Command in Berlin?'

He paused as if to allow Antonio the opportunity to voice an objection. 'Look, none of us are getting any younger and all we ask from anyone is to be left alone, to live out our lives without having to feel like hunted criminals.'

'Whether you like it or not,' Herman said. 'You've got the face of a German. You should be proud of it, and yes, of your father as well. What runs in your veins is German blood and that makes you one of us. So if you betray us, you betray yourself.'

Antonio crossed his arms to let them know he wasn't buying any of it.

'Perhaps if I explain to you how important our work is, and how much we wanted you to be a part of it,' Alfred said, 'you might — '

'Save your breath,' Antonio said. 'I only want to see my father. What you and your friends believe in is your business and has nothing to do with me. If you're worried that I'm going to make trouble for all of you, that's not why I came here.'

Alfred took a deep breath, exhaling slowly. 'You're a stubborn young man. I can see there is nothing we can say that will make you change your mind. You're determined to see your father, and we won't stand in your way. He's no longer at the address you gave the driver. He moved some time ago.'

'Where did he move to?'

'Don't worry, we'll make sure you get to see him,' Alfred said.

'When?'

'Soon,' Alfred replied. He stood up to bring their meeting to a close. 'Maybe in a day or two. Our driver will pick you up at your hotel and take you to him.'

They walked out of the seating area and stopped in front of the guillotine.

'You must admit,' Alfred said, his eyes focusing on the sharp blade glistening in the light of the room. 'It was a very ingenious invention. Very swift, very clean.'

'We could have used a few of them at Auschwitz,' Herman said.

His eyes still fixed on the blade, Alfred reached for a dangling cord and gave it a quick pull. The blade immediately dropped and severed the life-like head of Marie Antoinette. It rolled on to the floor and came to rest just inches away from Antonio.

'Make no mistake about it,' Alfred said firmly. 'We will not hesitate to do whatever is necessary to protect ourselves and our way of life. Do I make myself clear?'

'Perfectly,' Antonio said.

Alfred signalled to the two men who had abducted Antonio. 'You can take him back,' he said to them.

★ ★ ★

Alfred waited until the trio had made its way out of the cellar. 'What do you think, Herman? Did we overdo it?'

'I think it went reasonably well,' Herman said.

'Yes, perhaps too well,' Alfred said.

'What do you mean?'

'I'm not sure, but I have a feeling we may have to keep an eye on this young man for a long time to come. There's something about him. He was not what I expected — too sure of himself for one thing.'

'You worry too much, Alfred. I think after he sees the old man he'll be satisfied, and that will be the end of it.'

★ ★ ★

Shaken, Antonio stepped out of the cab and headed straight for the lounge and took a seat at the bar. 'Tequila,' he said to the bartender.

'Sí señor.'

'Make it a double,' Antonio added. 'And don't forget the lime.'

The bartender placed the tequila-filled glass on the counter along with a couple of wedges of lime and a salt shaker.

In almost ritualistic fashion, Antonio licked

the area behind his thumb and forefinger, sprinkled a little salt on it, licked it off and took a swig. He completed the process by sucking on a wedge of lime. He repeated it two more times to the amusement of an attractive young woman who entered the lounge and took a seat next to him.

'You're obviously Mexican,' she said, not too shyly. 'It's been a long time since I've seen someone drink tequila that way.'

'Yes, I am,' Antonio said. 'And you're obviously not Paraguayan. By your accent, I'd say you're Norwegian or possibly Danish.'

'Very good,' she said. 'I'm originally from Denmark but I've lived all over Europe.'

The bartender interrupted. 'What will you have today señorita?'

'I'll have a Scotch, straight up,' she said.

Antonio gave her a quick once-over. She had long, flowing blonde hair, ivory-smooth skin and a soft, seductive smile that reminded him of a young Lauren Bacall.

'Put that on my tab,' he told the bartender.

'Thank you,' she said. She opened her purse and pulled out a cigarette. 'I seem to be out of matches. Do you have a light?'

He reached into his pants pocket and produced a silver lighter. He struck it and brought it up to her cigarette.

She took a few quick puffs and exhaled

slowly to one side. 'Thanks, again,' she said.

The bartender placed her drink in front of her and turned to Antonio. 'Another tequila, señor?'

'Sure, why not,' he said.

She picked up her drink, took a sip, then said, 'By the way, my name is Ivana. I'm not usually this friendly with strangers, in case you're wondering.'

Antonio waited for the bartender to pour the tequila.

'I'm Antonio and now that we've met, I guess we're no longer strangers,' he said with a smile.

She smiled back and took another sip of her drink. 'Is this your first time in Paraguay?'

'Yes, I arrived yesterday. I'm here on . . . business; and you?'

'Just passing through. Actually, I was supposed to meet an old friend that I hadn't seen in years. I wanted to surprise her. When I got here, I discovered she had moved to Rio de Janeiro. I missed her by only a few days. So, I've decided to spend the rest of the week here, maybe do a little shopping and some sightseeing.'

They spent the next half hour talking and getting to know each other. It was exactly what Antonio needed to take his mind off his troubles. She was a little more aggressive than what he was used to, but under the circumstances, it really didn't matter. He offered no objections when she put her hand on his arm and said, 'I have a special bottle of cognac in my room just waiting to be opened.' He smiled knowingly and quickly asked for the bill.

★ ★ ★

Antonio had a satisfied grin on his face as he got off the bed and began to put on his pants. It had been fast and furious. Her choice, not his. Personally, he would've preferred to take his time, perhaps over a glass or two of cognac. But Ivana was the kind of woman who liked her sex like she liked her drinks, straight up and without preliminaries.

Ivana rolled across the bed and took her time getting up. She was naked except for a red, silk scarf around her neck, a fetish, she admitted, that helped turn her on.

'Maybe we can do it again later on,' she said, tugging on her scarf playfully. She sauntered across the room to the bathroom. 'I think I'll take a quick shower. Why don't you pour us a drink. The cognac is on top of the dresser.'

'Sure,' Antonio said with a smile. He saw the bottle of cognac and a couple of glasses sitting on top of the dresser. Off to one side, near the corner edge, was Ivana's purse with its strap dangling freely. He walked over to the dresser, picked up the bottle and began to fill each glass. A few drops spilled on to the dresser and he reached for a paper napkin. As he began to wipe it clean, he accidentally knocked the purse off the dresser. Some of the items spilled out and he quickly gathered them, one by one, and placed them back in the purse. He paused when he picked up a gold-plated lighter with the initials GSD engraved on one side. He struck it and it worked perfectly. He returned the purse to its original place, just as Ivana was coming out of the bathroom with a towel wrapped around her. He walked up to her and handed her a glass of cognac.

'Do you mind?' she said as she pulled off the towel and asked him to finish drying her off.

'Not at all,' he said with a tinge of coolness in his voice.

10

It was an unceremonious funeral. Simple, and without the usual litany of long-winded eulogies and prayers. It was the kind of funeral that Harry would have wanted. Except for his daughter, Pamela, most of the people who showed up to pay their respects were older people. Among them were a few Holocaust survivors who wept openly, as much for the loss of their friend as for the knowledge that their special group of tortured souls had been reduced by one.

★　★　★

'Thank you for coming, Mr Feldman,' Pamela said as she ushered the last of her father's mourners out of the apartment.

Across the room her mother was attempting to gather some dirty dishes and half-empty wine glasses.

'Leave it to me, mother. Why don't you just sit down and rest a while?'

'No, I have to keep busy. The place is a mess.' Suddenly a wine glass slipped from her hand and dropped to the floor where it broke into pieces. Unnerved, she let go of the other dishes and they all came crashing down around her. 'I'm not going to make it,' she said in a sudden burst of pent-up emotions. 'I'm not going to make it without him.' She cried uncontrollably.

Pamela rushed to put her arms around her. 'Of course you're going to make it. We're both going to make it and we're going to do it together. Daddy wouldn't want us to give up that easily. Besides, he's not really gone, you know.' She placed her hand over her mother's heart. 'He's in there, and he'll be there forever.'

Her mother sniffled as she tried to wipe away the tears from her face.

'What you need most is a good, restful nap,' Pamela said softly. 'After a couple of hours of sleep, you'll be surprised how much easier it will be to put things into perspective.' She walked her to the bedroom and helped her into bed.

'Perhaps you're right. I do need to rest a bit. Everything happened so fast. I couldn't sleep at all last night. My mind just kept racing over so many memories. Maybe now . . . maybe I can . . . ' Her voiced trailed off and she quickly fell asleep.

Pamela stepped quietly out of the room and went to clean up the broken dishes.

The quietness of the living room was just what she needed to take stock of everything that had to be done. There were lawyers and insurance agents to be contacted and funeral bills to be paid. She knew that her mother would expect her to handle these things.

She walked over to a beverage cart in the corner of the room and poured herself a glass of gin and club soda. Not exactly her preference, but it was that or a glass of overly-sweet wine. She was now ready to begin the unpleasant task of going through her father's personal papers.

Drink in hand, she made her way to her father's desk and sat down in his old swivel chair. She hadn't sat in the chair in years and it suddenly brought back memories of when she was a little girl. She remembered how her father used to pick her up and sit her down in the middle of the chair and spin her around. It used to be so much fun. She always protested when her father tried to take her off. One more time, Daddy, one more time, she used to say, and her daddy would always give in.

She took a sip of her drink. There would be time enough to look back and remember, she thought, her hand reaching up to wipe away a single tear that made its way half way down the side of her face. There was work to be done; the sooner she got started, the sooner she could begin to put it all behind her.

She pulled out the center drawer and sifted through a bunch of old papers and miscellaneous receipts. Any item which could be of possible value was removed and placed on top of the desk. She repeated the process with the rest of the drawers except for the bottom left drawer which was locked. As long as she could remember, her father had always kept that particular drawer locked. It was his personal drawer to which only he, and no one else, had access. She vaguely recalled that the few times she had observed her father open the drawer, he had retrieved the key from a nearby hiding place. She searched through every nook and cranny and found three keys, none of which fitted. Maybe he had removed the key and hidden it elsewhere in the apartment. She paused when she noticed a stack of tape cassettes sitting on the corner of the desk. One by one, she picked them up, opened them and put them aside. Holding the last one in her hand, she opened it and out came a brass-colored key that fell and bounced on top of the desk.

With child-like anticipation, she inserted the key in the locked drawer. It fitted perfectly. Stacked almost to the top were layers upon layers of old letters and faded newspaper clippings dating back to the end of World War II.

She combed through the material and began to read one news account after another. She read vivid descriptions of death camps like Dachau, Auschwitz, and about the gruesome experiments performed by the infamous Dr Josef Mengele. As she put down a piece about Adolf Eichmann, she asked herself why? Why did her father collect such articles? Maybe it helped him in some way to deal with his own pain, or maybe he planned on putting the articles in an album to give to some local Jewish organization. She would never know the real reason.

She skimmed through a few of the letters with postmarks from New York City, Los Angeles and several European cities. They were sad, nostalgic letters written by old friends, most of them Holocaust survivors, who seemed to have a special need to communicate with one another.

She came across her father's recent letter to the famous Nazi hunter, Meyer Bergman, and she read it with interest. Then she put it aside and wondered what her father had been up to.

As she continued to sift through the stack of articles and letters, she spotted a plain, gray notebook. The edges were tattered and there was no title or writing of any kind on its cover. She picked it up, took a long, deep breath and opened it slowly. The first entry was dated 18 June 1945. It was a long, rambling account of her father's efforts to find his Uncle Simon, the only other family member who had survived the Holocaust. The last few sentences summed up his feelings after learning that Simon had died in a hospital in Holland, just weeks after being rescued by American soldiers.

I feel so alone now. Uncle Simon has joined Father, Mother and Lisa. They have all gone to a better place. God forgive me, but sometimes I wish I had gone with them. It is not easy being the only one left behind.

She flipped to the next page and read an entry dated three weeks later. He wrote of his inability to sleep.

His face is forever etched in my mind. I wake up in the middle of the night, trembling and crying out for help. His cold, blue eyes, devoid of any emotion, look straight at me just moments before he pulls the trigger. It is the same, night after night. I pray to God for an end to these nightmares.

Pamela reached for a tissue to wipe away the tears and continued to read page after page. It was like looking into his soul. At times the depth and revelation of some of the entries were almost too much for her to bear. Yet, she kept on reading, unable to detach herself from the pain and sorrow that her father so vividly described.

Suddenly, the doorbell rang. She took a moment to compose herself.

'Good afternoon,' said a mild-looking old man. 'My name is David Liebermann. You must excuse me for being late. At my age I seem to lose track of everything, especially the time of day. I want to offer my condolences.'

'Please, come in,' Pamela said. She led him to the couch across the room. 'My mother is resting right now. She was so exhausted, poor thing. May I offer you a glass of wine, or a soft drink?'

'No, thank you. I know it's late. I just wanted to drop by to say how sorry I am, and to tell you and your mother that I share your loss because he was like a brother to me. If it hadn't been for your father . . . well, let's just say that he was a remarkable man. He stood

99

by me during a very difficult time in my life.'

'I take it you've known my father a long time,' Pamela said, taking a seat across from him.

'Yes. In fact, your father practically saved my life. It was shortly after my arrival in New York City. Someone I had known in Poland recognized me, and for reasons that are still not clear to me, began to spread vicious rumors that I had collaborated with the Nazis. One night a group of his friends cornered me and one of them started to beat me. Suddenly, out of nowhere, it seemed, your father appeared. He shouted to them to leave me alone. He defended me without knowing who I was or whether their accusations against me were true or not. From that moment, we became friends. Unfortunately, the years went by and we lost touch with one another.'

'It's a real comfort to listen to someone who knew my father from a long time ago,' she said.

The old man smiled politely.

'Did he ever talk about his experiences during the war?' she asked.

'Only after we got to know each other better. Sometimes, that was all he would talk about. I mean, about how the Nazis killed his family. The terrible memories were still fresh

100

in his mind and he felt frustrated and angry that no one had done anything about it. But more than anything, he felt guilt, survivor's guilt they call it now. He felt guilty for being the one to survive.'

'That explains a lot,' Pamela said. 'As a matter of fact, I can't recall a time when my father actually sat down with me and discussed anything to do with the war or the Holocaust. Looking back, I can only remember one instance when he said something to me, or rather in my presence. We were watching a TV newscast. It was about a Holocaust survivor who had committed suicide. He was one of those prisoners who worked inside the camp doing those awful, dreadful chores. Apparently, he carried the guilt throughout the years until he couldn't take it any longer and so he killed himself. My father became unusually upset and he left the room. He kept muttering something about how a man had no choice. And then the last thing he said was that he wished he had enough money so he could quit his job and devote his life to hunting down Nazis. It seemed out of character for him and later I mentioned it to my mother. She just shrugged it off and said it was probably something he needed to get off his chest.'

The old man nodded. 'It was only natural

for your father to react that way,' he said in a knowing manner. 'After all, he knew what it felt like to be shunned by his fellow prisoners for — '

She frowned slightly.

'I . . . I thought you knew,' he stuttered. 'Please forgive me.'

'Are you trying to tell me that my father was one of those prisoners?'

'I'm sorry, truly I am,' he said.

'But how can you be sure? Did my father actually confide in you about such a thing?'

'Like I said before, during a period of time your father seemed to want to talk about everything that had happened to him.'

Pamela became silent and after a few moments, the old man got up to leave.

'I'll see myself out,' he said. He managed a soft, almost inaudible, 'I'm sorry,' as he opened and closed the door behind him.

11

It had been a little over thirty-six hours since the two thugs had dropped Antonio off at the hotel. He had not heard from anyone and wondered why it was taking so long for them to contact him. Maybe they had changed their minds, or maybe they were just being cautious. He had intentionally avoided venturing too far from the hotel for fear he would miss a phone call. Twice he had run into Ivana, or whatever her name was, and each time he had managed a feeble excuse for not being able to get together with her.

He was stretched out on the bed with the TV on when he heard a knock on the door. It was almost midnight. Half asleep, he listened and heard it again. He quickly got up.

'Antonio de la Vega?' said a young, auburn-haired woman with a serious expression. She had slightly almond-shaped eyes and a wide, full-lipped mouth that gave her a pouty, sensual look. She was wearing a dark-colored dress that reached to the top of her thin, shapely knees.

'Yes,' he said, nodding.

'My name is Pamela Friedman. I'm Harry

Friedman's daughter. We spoke on the phone.'

'Yes, of course. But what are you doing here?'

'May I come in?'

'I'm sorry, please come in.'

She stepped inside and took a seat in front of a small table next to a window.

'You're the last person I expected to see at my door,' he said as he turned off the TV and joined her at the table. 'I'm sorry I couldn't attend the funeral but I had some important business to take care of here in Asunción.'

'I know my being here must seem very strange to you,' she said. 'After all, you don't even know me. But you knew my father, and that's why I'm here.'

'I'm not sure I understand.'

'After his funeral, I had to go over his personal papers and I came across some letters and a diary. It was very painful for me, but I learned a lot about him. For so many years he had kept the past to himself.'

'Then you know why I'm here,' he said.

She nodded. 'The last entries in the diary explained everything. And before I left Miami, my mother filled me in on the rest. She told me how my father had spotted you in the restaurant.'

'I see,' he said. 'But I still don't understand what — '

'What I'm doing here?' she said. 'I'm not really sure I have a good answer. It was just something that I had to do. That afternoon, I decided I wanted to carry on and finish what my father had begun. But there's more to it than that. It's really difficult to explain.'

'I can see it's going to be a long night,' Antonio said. 'Why don't we go downstairs? There's a quiet lounge where we can continue to talk.'

'Actually, I would prefer to go someplace where I can have a cup of tea,' she said.

'There's a coffee shop across the street.' He stood up, grabbed his coat from an easy chair in the corner and led the way out of the room.

★　★　★

'How did you know where I was staying?' Antonio said. They were standing in the hallway waiting for the elevator.

'It really wasn't that difficult. I looked it up in a South America travel guide. There weren't that many hotels in Asunción. I called though, just to make certain.'

The elevator door opened and he stepped in ahead of her and pressed the L button.

'I wasn't sure what your reaction would be,' she said. 'But somehow I had a feeling that you would at least be sympathetic. My father trusted you and that was good enough for me.' They glanced up and saw the light move quickly from one number to the next. The 'L' indicator lit up and the door opened to the main lobby, and to the sight of Ivana who was waiting to go up.

Antonio gave her a curt smile and a cool hello.

'Hello, Antonio,' she said flirtingly. 'We seem to run into each other a lot, don't we?' She entered the elevator as Antonio and Pamela stepped onto the lobby floor.

'Yes . . . well, it was nice seeing you,' Antonio said. 'I'll call you when I get a chance.'

'Please do. You know my room number.' The door closed and Antonio and Pamela walked off.

'Friend of yours?' Pamela asked.

'No . . . I mean, I met her in the bar. We had a few drinks together, that's all.'

Pamela smiled. They walked out of the hotel, crossed the street and entered the coffee shop. They took the only available table next to the kitchen. A waitress in a plain, white uniform walked up to their table to take their order.

'Two cups of tea,' Antonio said.

Pamela had a lot on her mind and it showed.

'I don't know how to explain why I'm here,' she said. 'So much has happened the past two days. I guess I'm here because . . . it's really hard for me to say this. But I want to see him, face to face, the man who murdered my father's family. After reading all those letters about the Nazis and the Holocaust, I knew I had to do something, and the first thing that came to mind was to finish what my father had started.'

'I understand how you feel,' he said, 'but you should know that these people who have protected my father over the years are dangerous, and they wouldn't hesitate to kill either one of us. For your safety I think you should get on the first flight back to Miami.'

'I appreciate your concern, but I'm staying,' she said. 'There's nothing you can say that'll make me change my mind.'

The waitress placed the two cups of tea on the table. 'Will there be anything else?' she asked.

'Thank you, that'll be all,' Antonio said.

Pamela continued. 'I'd like to believe that my father would have wanted me to be here. Although, to be honest, he never discussed his past. It may seem strange to you, but I really didn't know what he had gone through and how much he suffered until I read his diary. He kept it a secret all these years. I know now that it probably had to do with the fact he felt a certain amount of guilt for what he had to do in the prison camp.'

Antonio leaned forward. 'What did he do?'

'He was one of those prisoners who was forced to do the unpleasant tasks, like carrying the dead bodies to the mass graves and things like that. He probably did this for only a short period of time, but the guilt stayed with him the rest of his life. I know from reading about the Holocaust that people who did these things were usually allowed to live a little longer, and that was their reward, if you want to call it that.'

'Did he write about it in his diary?'

'No, as a matter of fact, it was an old friend of his who told me about it the day of the funeral. He inadvertently let it slip. He didn't mean to tell me, but I'm glad it came out. It explains why my father never wanted to talk about his past or about the Holocaust. It's really too bad because I would have understood, and it probably would have brought us closer to each other.'

'You weren't that close, I take it.'

'Well, we were close at times, but at other times we were very much at odds. Looking back, I guess the main reason my father and I drifted apart was because I wasn't as Jewish as he wanted me to be. If only he had talked to me about his experiences I might've been more religious . . . who knows?'

Antonio looked at her, thoughtfully. 'Your father once asked me this question and now I'm going to ask you the same question. When you meet Schumann, what then?'

'I don't know,' she said, shaking her head. 'I really hadn't thought about it. I just wanted to be here in case you do find him. But don't worry, I won't do anything rash, like try to shoot him. Not that the thought didn't cross my mind.'

'Good,' Antonio said. 'Now that we've got that out of the way, let me fill you in on what I've been able to find out.'

He described everything that happened to him from the time he went searching for clues in Queretaro, to his trip to El Paso and finally, to his arrival in Asunción. He held nothing back and felt a sense of relief that he was no longer alone. With Friedman gone, it seemed fitting that his daughter, Pamela, would be there to share the moment when he came face to face with his father.

'I'm afraid there's not much we can do until we hear from them,' he said.

'What if they refuse to allow me to accompany you?'

'I'll insist. They may not like it but I want them to know that you have as much right to meet him as I do.'

'Let me ask you something,' she said. 'What do you plan to do after we meet him? I mean are we just going to walk away and forget we saw him?'

'I haven't decided. Though I agree that we can't simply walk away from it.'

'Well, then I think we should call Meyer Bergman.'

Antonio hesitated. 'I don't know . . . I think maybe we're moving too fast with this. I mean, why don't we wait until — '

'Sounds like you have mixed feelings. You do want to see him brought to justice, don't you?'

'Of course I do,' he said defensively. 'But you're right, we must be ready to provide Bergman with everything we learn about him. What he did to your father's family is unforgivable, and he must be held accountable.' He took a sip of his tea and moved the cup to one side. 'Maybe tomorrow will be the day,' he said, signalling for the check.

★ ★ ★

110

Peter spotted them from behind the counter and pretended not to notice them. When he saw them step into the elevator, he picked up the phone and dialled Herman's number.

'Hello,' said a groggy-sounding Herman.

'It's me, Peter.'

'For God's sake, it's past midnight. You better have a good reason for getting me out of bed.'

'I just saw Antonio with a young woman. She checked in a little over an hour ago.'

'So what's the urgency? It's late and — '

'She registered under the name Pamela Friedman, from Miami Beach.'

There was a long silence.

'Herman, did you hear me? I said — '

'I heard you, I was just trying to figure out what the hell she's doing here. She must be Friedman's daughter.'

'What do you want me to do?'

'Nothing, absolutely nothing.'

'But Herman, she is obviously here for the same reason that Antonio is, to see the old man.'

'I told you, don't do anything.'

'Well, if that's how you feel. But I'll keep my eye on her, just in case.'

'You do that, Peter. Now let me go back to sleep.'

The line went dead.

★ ★ ★

Pamela had just begun to undress when she heard a knock on the door. She quickly buttoned her collar and walked across the room to look through the viewer. She saw a pudgy, middle-aged man standing to one side.

'Who is it?' she asked.

'I'm a friend of your father's,' said the man. 'I know it's late but it's important that I speak with you.'

She cautiously opened the door and allowed him to introduce himself.

'My name is Leonard Rosenberg. I didn't mean to disturb you. I know why you came here and I thought that you might need my help. If you'll allow me to come in, I'll be glad to explain.'

He seemed harmless enough, she thought. Besides, she was curious.

'Come in, but only for a moment. I'm really very tired.'

He walked in and sat down on a small couch. She sat on a chair across from him.

'You said you knew my father.'

'I met him years ago. In Miami Beach, in fact. I wasn't really a friend of his. We just happened to be in the same room during a fund-raising for the Holocaust Memorial.'

'But why did you — '

'Please, let me explain. I only said that I was his friend because I figured you wouldn't turn me away that easily.'

'Well, you figured right. I'm listening.'

'Let me begin by saying that I'm very sorry about your loss. I know that being an only child must make it very difficult to — '

'How did you know I was an only child?'

'My associates in Miami furnished me with a brief — and I emphasize brief — report on you. Like the Aryan Knights, which you may have heard about, we have eyes and ears everywhere. You see, I belong to the JFJ, Jews for Justice, a small group of dedicated Jews who are committed to locating Nazi fugitives in South America.'

'Then you must be working with Meyer Bergman and his organization.'

'Not exactly. The truth is, although we share the same objectives, our methods are different and, we feel, more effective.'

'I'm afraid I don't understand. Why should there be any differences if the only objective is to locate and bring these murderers to justice?'

'I'm glad you used the word justice because it is precisely where Bergman's group and ours differ. Everyone agrees that every effort should be made to locate these monsters. But then what happens to them after they're caught? A long, costly trial. For what? They're guilty. We know that. Everyone knows that. Yes, we believe in bringing them to justice. But we believe it should be swift and without formalities.'

'Are you trying to say that your purpose in locating them is . . . to kill them?'

There was a brief pause. 'We prefer the word 'execute'. Does it shock you? It shouldn't. We are, after all, only interested in carrying out a sentence they would probably receive if they were arrested and sent back to Europe or some other place. Some might even say we are doing the world a favor. But truthfully, we don't care whether or not people agree with our methods. We are determined to do what we feel is necessary until there is not a single Nazi fugitive left in the world.'

Pamela leaned back and folded her arms. She didn't quite know what to make of Rosenberg. She was a little disturbed but at the same time intrigued.

'You obviously know that I came here to join Antonio de la Vega. And I assume that your reason for telling me this is that you want me to help you. But to be honest, I'm not sure if I agree with your philosophy. And even if I did, I'm certain that Antonio would

114

not go along with it.'

'I was hoping to keep this conversation between us,' he said. 'Let's face it, Antonio is not only a gentile, but he's also German. Blood runs very deep and no matter what Antonio says to you right now, in the end he'll side with his father. Believe me, I know what I'm talking about.'

Pamela relaxed her arms. 'You're wrong. He has no feelings whatsoever for Schumann. It's not like he's a teenager looking for his long-lost father. Besides, whether or not I tell him anything is my decision.'

Rosenberg stood up. 'Look, all I'm asking is that you tell me where I can find him,' Rosenberg said. 'Do it for your father, you owe him that much.'

He reached into his shirt pocket and pulled out a piece of paper with his name and phone number scribbled on it. 'We're counting on you,' he said, handing it to her. 'Don't let us down.' He abruptly turned and walked out of the room.

Pamela remained seated. She didn't quite know what to make of Rosenberg and his means-justifies-the-end philosophy. She had always assumed that such people represented an extremism that most mainstream Jews did not endorse. But could it be that some of these same Jews secretly supported the efforts of groups like the JFJ? She wondered, and she wondered about Antonio. Perhaps Rosenberg was right. Blood was everything and maybe, just maybe, it would cause Antonio to have second thoughts about turning in his father. For the time being, she would say nothing to him about her conversation with Rosenberg.

★　★　★

Rosenberg stepped off the elevator and went directly to a room in the middle of the hall. He looked to his right, then to his left, then knocked. Soon, he heard the sound of someone coming to answer the door.

'Who is it?' said a muffled-sounding voice.

'It's me, Leonard.'

The door opened and Rosenberg quickly stepped inside the room. Ivana's face was barely visible as she shut the door behind him.

12

The waiter poured coffee for Antonio and hot tea for Pamela. 'How did you sleep?' Antonio asked.

'Pretty well for the first few hours,' Pamela said. 'But then I suddenly woke up and couldn't go back to sleep. Too much anxiety, I guess.'

'I slept okay, but I know what you mean about the anxiety. I just wish they would call me. I don't know why they're taking so long. At first, I thought they wanted to keep an eye on me to find out if I had come alone. But now, I'm not so sure.'

'While I was awake last night, I started thinking about your father, about what will happen to him later on. Have you thought about it? I mean, about the possibility that he will have to face an execution?'

'What made you ask that?' he asked, suspiciously.

'I don't know. I just thought you should think about it, considering he is your father.'

Antonio took a deep breath. 'Somehow I feel you're not entirely convinced that I will do what I have to do. Believe me, I have no illusions about my father. As a matter of fact — '

'Excuse me,' said a soft-spoken man who walked up to their table. 'I'm here to take you to your father.'

Antonio recognized him as the driver of the cab that had taken him to the mansion.

'I've been expecting you. But I want you to know that this lady is coming with me,' he said, nodding towards Pamela.

The driver looked at her and said, 'Very well. Please follow me. My cab is just outside.'

Antonio and Pamela looked at each other, surprised the driver had offered no objections. They stood up, left some money on the table and followed him out of the restaurant.

'How far is this place you're taking us to?' Antonio asked as they got into the cab.

'I'm sorry,' the driver said, 'but my instructions were to take you to your father and not have any conversation with you.' After they had pulled away from the hotel, he added, 'It's not very far from here.'

Neither Antonio nor Pamela said very much as they sat back and looked out the windows of the cab. The streets and houses reminded Antonio of Mexico City and made him think of his mother. He had meant to call her before leaving the city, but it was just as well that he didn't. He wouldn't have known what to say.

* * *

The cab driver was right. It was only a short drive from the hotel.

'This is it,' he said turning into the semi-circular driveway of a white, colonial style building.

'There must be some mistake,' Antonio said, looking at the sign above the entrance. It read Sanitorio El Paraiso.

'I'm sorry, but there's no mistake. Your father is here. When you go inside someone will help you. If you wish, I will wait for you.'

Antonio and Pamela looked at each other. They got out of the cab, then walked inside. They were greeted by a matronly nurse dressed in a white uniform with a name tag over her left breast-pocket that said Paula Cervantes.

'Welcome to Sanitorio El Paraiso,' she said with a courteous smile. 'Are you here to visit a loved one?'

'We're here to visit my . . . a gentleman by the name of Hans Schumann,' Antonio said.

'Oh, yes,' she said. 'We were told someone would be visiting him today. If you will follow me, I will show you to his room.'

119

She led the way past a set of swinging doors, down a long corridor filled with the sounds and smells of a typical nursing home. On either side of the hallway were sad, pathetic-looking people in wheelchairs. Most were old, but a few were young. One old man with a scraggly, white beard and a large protruding growth over his right eye suddenly tried to grab Pamela.

'Please, help me,' he yelled over and over again. Pamela instinctively withdrew and continued walking. The old man yelled even louder and soon others joined in with pleas of their own. Their cries quickly reached a crescendo that stopped only when the trio exited the corridor and the door shut behind them.

'Poor souls,' the nurse said matter-of-factly. 'They are the charity cases. We do the best we can.'

They walked across an open garden of neatly trimmed trees, bushes and flowers. Evidence of a gardener's care was everywhere, especially in the way a group of exceptionally large, perfect roses was planted in the center of the yard. Off to one side was a three-foot statue of St Francis of Assisi. Next to it was a simple bird bath where a single sparrow was busy drinking water. The trio walked past the statue and entered a corridor of a wing reserved for the wealthy. In contrast to the corridor they had just left, this hallway was impeccably clean and bright. A quick glance at the rooms revealed that the mostly elderly residents were given the best of care. Some had private nurses by their bedsides, watching over them or reading out loud to them.

The nurse stopped just short of the open doorway to Schumann's room and cautioned them not to expect too much from him.

'His progress has been rather slow,' she said. 'Maybe seeing you will help somehow. Strokes are very unpredictable and it is difficult to say how much improvement he will make in the months to come.'

'Stroke,' Antonio said. 'How . . . bad is he?'

'His left side is completely paralyzed and so far he's been unable to speak. If you need any assistance, the nurse at the end of the hall will be glad to help you.' She smiled politely and turned back towards the courtyard.

Antonio and Pamela shared a quick moment of shock.

'I don't know if I can go in there,' Antonio said, shaking his head. 'I mean, what's the point?'

Pamela put her hand on his shoulder. 'Look, I know how you feel. But we've come this far. I think you should at least meet him.

You'll probably regret it later if you don't go in there.'

'What about you?' he asked.

She shook her head. 'To go in and try to talk to him, knowing that he can't respond . . . it's like everything bad that I had secretly wished on him has come true. I agree that it's all over. But you, you still have to face the fact that as evil as he once was, he's still your father.'

'You're right,' he said, his voice tense. 'I've got to face him.' He stepped up to the doorway and quietly entered the room.

Schumann was sitting in a wheelchair facing a window with a view of a small pond surrounded by a large, grassy area. There were ducks swimming in the pond, and their quacking sounds were faintly audible. Antonio approached softly and stopped just off to one side where Schumann could see him from the corner of his eye. Like a frightened child, he called out to him, 'Mister Schumann. I've . . . I've come a long way to see you. My name is Antonio de la Vega.'

Schumann's eyes slowly followed him as Antonio stepped closer and came around to face him. The left side of his thin, pale face drooped slightly, especially around his eye, which was partially obscured by thick glasses that seemed too big for his face. His neatly

122

combed hair, receding at the temples, was white, except for thin streaks of gray towards the crown.

'Look at me,' Antonio said, a bitter edge to his voice. 'Look at my face. Don't you recognize your own son? I'm from Mexico City. The same place you met my mother thirty years ago.' He paused and waited for some kind of acknowledgement, a nod, a blink, anything. But Schumann just stared at him without emotion.

Antonio briefly looked away. For a second, he was tempted to leave without saying another word.

When he turned back, he was struck by what he saw. Schumann's eyes were filled with tears. He swallowed hard and wiped away the moistness from his own eyes.

'Look, I know that my being here must be a shock to you, but I had to see you, face to face. It was only recently that I learned who you were. Before that, all I knew was what my mother told me from the time I was a little boy. Looking back, some of the things she said were not very convincing. But she wanted me to accept the story she created and I guess I just went along with it.'

Schumann listened and kept his reddened eyes focused on Antonio.

'I want you to know that it hasn't been easy

for me to meet you,' Antonio said. 'I'll probably never see you again and I'm not sure whether I'll tell my mother that I spoke to you.'

Schumann blinked a few times and caused the tears to flow down the sides of his face. He had the look of a wounded animal that wanted only to be left alone.

'Goodbye,' Antonio said as he abruptly turned and walked out of the room.

'It was much harder than I expected,' he said, shaking his head. 'He was so helpless, so . . . so pitiful. Let's get out of here.'

★ ★ ★

Pamela sat on the edge of the bed and dialled the number from the piece of paper Rosenberg had given her. He should know, she thought, that Schumann's physical condition had reduced him to a helpless old man of no further consequence to anyone.

'Hello?' he answered.

'Mister Rosenberg?'

'Speaking.'

'It's Pamela. I just wanted to let you know that Antonio and I just got back from seeing Schumann. Unfortunately it was not what we — '

'Where is he?'

'We were taken to a nursing home called El Paraiso just a few miles from here.'

'You actually saw him and talked to him?'

'Well, only Antonio got to meet him. You see, when we got there we found that Schumann had suffered a stroke that left him paralyzed on one side and unable to speak. He's been in that condition for almost a year and a half. To be honest, I'm still in shock. I just never expected that our search would end like this.'

'You did well in calling me. He's one less Nazi that we have to concern ourselves with. Thank you.' He abruptly hung up and left Pamela wondering whether she had done the right thing.

★ ★ ★

Antonio spotted Pamela sitting at a table off to the side of the bar. She was sipping a glass of white wine.

'It's been a hell of a day,' he said as he walked up and took a seat across from her. He signalled to the bartender to bring him a glass of wine. 'I'll be glad when I'm out of this city, away from everything that's happened today. I made reservations for a flight leaving at three. How about you?'

'I'm booked on a two o'clock flight.'

'Good, we can take a cab together. What are your plans? I mean, when you get back to Miami?'

'I'm not really sure, but I think I want to become involved in activities that promote an awareness of the Holocaust. I want to do it, not only for the sake of my father's memory, but also for myself. I'm not going to become fanatical about it, but it's the least I can do. Before, I used to worry about my job, my social life, having the right kind of clothes . . . well, you know what I'm trying to say.'

The waiter appeared with the glass of wine and placed it in front of Antonio.

'What about you?' she asked. 'What are you going to do?'

'I don't know yet. I'm still in a daze. I can't get the sight of my father sitting in that wheelchair out of my mind. In a way I'm relieved that it won't be necessary to notify Bergman about him. I mean, there would be no point. He's already imprisoned by his paralysis.'

'There's something you should know,' she said, haltingly. 'Last night, after we went up to our rooms, I was visited by a man who belongs to an anti-Nazi organization called the JFJ. His name is Leonard Rosenberg. Somehow he knew I had come here to help

126

you locate Schumann. At first I thought he might be involved in the same type of work that Bergman and his organization are famous for. But I quickly found out that their objective is very different. The JFJ seeks only to . . . to kill the ex-Nazis they find. As you might guess, he wanted me to let him know the moment I found out where Schumann was living. Anyway, he requested that I not tell you anything. He thought you might — '

'He thought I might warn my father, is that it?' Antonio said, harshly. 'I'm a little disappointed. I mean, I thought we had an understanding. Apparently I was wrong.'

'No, you weren't wrong and I'm sorry I didn't tell you about it this morning. You have every right to be upset with me. But there's more.'

'What do you mean more?'

'Well, after we got back from the nursing home, I called Rosenberg and told him all about it. I just thought that if he knew about Schumann's physical condition, he would forget about wanting to kill him.'

Antonio shook his head. 'Are there any more surprises?'

'Look, I'm sorry it happened that way, but you have to admit, you and I aren't exactly long-time friends. I know very little about you and unfortunately I allowed Rosenberg to place that small doubt about you in my head. Again, all I can say is I'm sorry.'

'Forget it. Maybe it's just as well that others know about him. It shouldn't be a secret, after all these years. He's my father, but he's also a war criminal who has no right to expect any privacy. I just hope that any media reports about him are played down because I'm not sure what I'm going to tell my mother.' He picked up his glass and took a quick gulp.

'I . . . guess after today we'll probably never see each other again. But just in case you ever make it to Miami, I want to give you my phone number.' She rummaged through her purse for something to write on and found the piece of paper that Rosenberg had given her.

'I'll write it on the back of this,' she said. 'I doubt I'll ever have to use it again.' She wrote her name and phone number on the small piece of paper and handed it to Antonio.

'Thanks,' he said, stuffing it in his coat pocket. 'You never know when a client will ask to meet me in Miami.'

★　★　★

Herman picked up the phone and dialled Alfred's number at the mansion. It was busy. He tried again a few minutes later and got through.

'It's me, Herman. I thought you should know about Antonio and the young woman.'

'Well, what is it?'

'Peter at the hotel called me and said they had checked out. They took a cab to the airport.'

'Good,' Alfred said.

'Personally, I think we shouldn't have let him go so easily,' Herman said. 'He knows too much about us. And that young woman. I just don't trust her.'

'Well, don't worry about it. They came to see Schumann and we didn't try to stop them. Did we? I don't think either one of them will want to come back anytime soon.'

'I hope you're right,' Herman said. 'I hope you're right.'

★   ★   ★

It was a little after 1.30 p.m. when the boarding call for Pamela's flight came over the loudspeaker.

'Well, this is it,' she said as they stood up to

129

say their final goodbye. 'I don't know if I did the right thing by coming here, but I'm glad I got to meet you. Whoever would have thought that my father's chance encounter with you in that restaurant would lead to all of this? It's going to take a while for me to come down to reality.' She paused to wipe away a tear from the side of her cheek. 'I never really got a chance to grieve for my father, and I'm afraid that once I get back to Miami, I'm going to fall apart.'

'I want you to know that I feel lucky to have met your father,' Antonio said. 'And you're right, if it hadn't been for his persistence from the day he first saw me, I wouldn't have discovered the truth about my own father and . . . I wouldn't have met you. I only wish it had been under different circumstances.'

She smiled and gave him a quick kiss on the cheek. 'Take care of yourself, and good luck with your mother.' She turned and walked toward a short line of passengers waiting to board the plane.

Antonio watched her for a few seconds, then suddenly called out.

'Pamela, wait.'

She turned.

He wanted to tell her that he hoped they could keep in touch, just to talk, just to stay friends. But he stopped himself and waved goodbye to her, instead.

She waved back at him and turned to join the others, moving quickly towards the open doorway.

13

It was almost midnight when the cab dropped Antonio off in front of Dr Pacheco's residence in the exclusive Polanco area of Mexico City. He hoped the doctor would still be up.

'Please come in,' the housekeeper said, opening the door. 'He's in the study. I'll tell him you're here.'

Dr Pacheco soon appeared and greeted Antonio with a handshake and a hearty embrace.

'It's good to see you, Antonio. Nothing's wrong, I hope.'

'No, nothing's wrong. But there is something I need to discuss with you, if it's not too late.'

'Of course not. Come, let's make ourselves comfortable and you can tell me what this is all about.' They walked to the study and sat in two identical leather chairs with a matching leather-topped table between them. In the center of the table was a half-empty bottle of brandy surrounded by four crystal snifters. 'Can I offer you a brandy?'

'No, thank you. It's late and I really don't

want to take up too much of your time.'

'By the look on your face I can guess this has something to do with your father.'

'How did you know? Have you been talking to my mother?'

Dr Pacheco nodded. 'You must understand that I've known your mother a long time, even before you were born. She had no one else to turn to and so she came to me and told me everything. I wasn't surprised, though. I always knew that some day you would learn the truth about your father. She wanted to tell you, but as you got older she kept putting it off. And then she just decided to let it stay in the past. She did it as much for herself as for you.'

'Then you've known all along about my real father and you never said anything.'

'Yes, and believe me, it wasn't easy for me to keep up the pretence. But it was your mother's decision, and I had to go along with it.'

Antonio paused for a moment. 'I think I'll have that brandy after all.'

Dr Pacheco picked up the bottle and poured a little under two fingers into two snifters. He handed one to Antonio and picked up the other one for himself.

'*Salud*,' he said half-heartedly. He took a quick sip and placed his glass on the table.

Antonio held on to his and kept it next to his chest.

'To be honest, I'm glad that it's all out in the open,' Dr Pacheco said. 'I'm just sorry you had to learn about your father the way you did.'

'In a way I'm relieved that my mother confided in you. This will make it easier for me to discuss the problem that I'm facing. As my mother probably already told you, I left a few days ago without giving her much of an explanation as to where I was going or what I planned to do. I was later joined by a young woman, the daughter of the old man who first got me involved in all of this. It took a while, but I did find my father. He's living in Paraguay.'

'Did you speak to him?' Dr Pacheco asked.

'Yes, and that's what I want to talk to you about. After my brief meeting with him, I started to think about my mother and whether I should tell her about it.' He shook his head. 'It was . . . absolutely the worst experience of my life. I had gone there to see him with the idea that . . . no, with the intention of making him feel guilty for the way he had abandoned my mother. But when I saw him sitting in that wheelchair, I just went numb. He had suffered a stroke that left him paralyzed and unable to speak. You can

134

imagine how I felt.'

Dr Pacheco took a sip of brandy. 'I see the problem. You don't know if you should tell your mother that the man she loved so many years ago is now a sick, helpless old man. Well, I wish I could tell you that it's all in the past and that she wouldn't be affected if you tell her about it. But, the fact is, she was hopelessly in love with him.'

'Then you must have known him.'

'Not really. I saw him once when he and your mother were sitting on a bench in Alameda Park. At the time, I was very fond of your mother. We dated a few times and I had always hoped it would develop into something more serious.'

'I don't know what to say, Doctor Pacheco. You always did give my mother special attention. And those late night calls from time to time. I should have figured it out.'

'I want you to know that it wasn't easy for me to see your mother heart-broken and pregnant after your father left so suddenly. Of course, I offered to marry her, not just to give you my name, but because I really loved her. But she wouldn't even consider it. All her young girl illusions were shattered and it affected her in a way that made her shy away from all men, even to this day.'

'You're still in love with my mother, aren't you?'

Dr Pacheco hesitated. 'Yes, I suppose I am. But not in the way you think. What I mean to say is that over the years I've come to appreciate her as a woman of great fortitude for whom I would do anything. She's always known that she can count on me, and I'm happy with that. But enough about me. Let's talk about what we're going to do.'

'After everything you've told me,' Antonio said, 'I'm more confused than ever. She's very intelligent as you well know, and I've got to tell her something that she will accept, that she can live with.'

'Well, no matter what you tell her, it's going to hurt her in a way that neither you nor I can understand. My advice is that you tell her the truth . . . up to a point.'

'You think I should tell her that I actually saw him and talked to him?'

'Yes. Tell her that you had a very brief meeting with your father. But don't, under any circumstances, tell her about his physical condition. It would absolutely crush her.'

Antonio took a sip of his brandy and placed the glass next to him on the table. 'Then it's settled. I'll tell her that I met my father and . . . hmm . . . I'm going to have to make something up, though, like what he told me, what we talked about and — '

'You'll have to sound convincing. I suggest you skip the details. Give it some thought and try not to over-embellish. And whatever you do, make certain she knows that you have no intention of ever seeing your father again.'

'I understand,' Antonio said, nodding. 'I think I'll sleep on it and maybe wait a day or two before telling her anything. For now, I just need to unwind. Maybe someday we can talk some more, not just about my mother but about other things.'

'I'll look forward to it,' Dr Pacheco said with a quiet smile.

They stood up, shook hands and made their way to the front door.

'Can I call a cab for you?' Dr Pacheco asked.

'It won't be necessary. I told the driver to wait.'

They exchanged goodbyes and simultaneously reached out to hug one another.

14

The next morning, Antonio answered the door and saw his mother standing there with a serious look on her face.

'Mother . . . what are you doing here?'

'Doctor Pacheco called me a little while ago and I thought it would be best if we talked in person.' She walked in and took a seat on the couch.

'What did he tell you?' he asked as he approached her and gave her a quick peck on the cheek. He sat down beside her.

'He really didn't say much. But I could tell something was not right. I asked if it had to do with you and he reluctantly said that you had dropped by to see him last night. I tried to press him about what the two of you had talked about, but he refused to say anything.' She paused, then said, 'You found him, didn't you?'

Antonio reached for her hand and squeezed it gently. 'Yes,' he said softly. 'I didn't call you last night because I had to give myself time to think, to let it all sink in. He's living in Paraguay.'

'Did you meet him, talk to him?'

'I introduced myself to him, and I talked to him, or at least I tried to talk to him. The shock of meeting me may have been too much for him because he had very little to say. He was obviously uncomfortable and said that he needed time to accept the fact he had a grown son.'

'Did he . . . ask about me?'

Antonio gave her a reassuring nod. 'He asked how you were and . . . if you had married.'

'That's it? Surely he must have said more than that.'

'Like I said, he was very uncomfortable, and he really didn't want to continue our conversation. The truth is, I was just as uncomfortable, and I didn't know what else to say or do. Maybe it was best that we left it the way we did.' Antonio had never been a good liar and didn't want to trip himself by saying too much. 'I'm sorry mother, I know how you must feel. I wish I could — '

She suddenly broke into tears.

Antonio reached to put his arms around her. 'It's okay, mother, it's okay.'

'You don't understand,' she said, shaking her head. 'After all these years, not knowing whether he was dead or alive, to suddenly have to relive the past . . . '

Hans Schumann took his usual seat in front of a fountain in the middle of Alameda Park. He was impeccably dressed in a dark, wool suit that, along with his fine European features, made him stand out from among the local visitors to the park. He had a habit of glancing at his watch as he waited for Elena to arrive. Moments later, the girl appeared and took a seat next to him.

'I'm sorry I was a little late,' she said, 'but the store manager wanted me to put some things away before I took my break.'

'I understand. I only wish I could see you some other time when you don't have to worry about having to go back to work. Have you thought about what I said? I mean, about trying to find some time in the evening or the weekend? I'd really like to take you out to dinner some day, and maybe afterwards go someplace where we can dance.'

She smiled. 'As a matter of fact, I've given it a lot of thought, and I think I've come up with a way we can spend at least part of an evening together.'

'You have?' he said, mildly surprised.

'My friend, Teresa, and I have joined a library study group that meets once a week, on Friday evenings between eight and ten.

She's a good friend, and I know I can count on her to cover for me.'

'Well, if that's the only way we can enjoy an evening together, then that's the way it will have to be,' he said. 'But promise that you'll consider introducing me to your parents so we won't have to be so secretive.'

She suddenly became serious. 'You know I would like nothing more than to have you come to my house. But I know my father very well and I know he would order me to stop seeing you. He has very old ideas about the kind of young men I should go out with. I just don't want to risk spoiling what we have. So, please, Hans, let's just take it one day at a time.'

'You're right,' he said. 'I keep forgetting I'm in a Latin country.' He smiled and leaned over to give her a quick, awkward kiss.

'By the way,' she said. 'You're not still thinking of leaving Mexico City, are you? If it's a question of finding a job, there are plenty of opportunities here.'

'It has nothing to do with finding a job,' he said cautiously. 'I just never considered staying here for more than a few weeks. The fact is, ever since I met you, I simply put all my plans on hold. Nothing would please me more than to be able to stay here for ever.'

'Does that mean you'll consider looking for

something permanent?' she said, her eyes bright with excitement.

He was reluctant to give her a definite answer. 'You know, it's not going to be that easy for an ex-soldier like myself to find a position. And being a foreigner who can barely speak Spanish, well, I just don't know.'

'But you'll give it a try, won't you?' she said insistently.

He gave in to her and said, 'Okay, maybe tomorrow I'll look around to see what's available.'

She smiled and gave out a quiet sigh.

'You know,' she said. 'You've never told me about what you did in the war. It must have been a terrible experience.'

Hans stiffened. 'What made you say that?'

'I was just curious. It must be very painful for you to talk about it. If you'd rather not, I understand.'

'No, it's not that. It's . . . well, if you must know. My entire military career was spent behind a desk. I was a junior officer in charge of providing supplies and equipment to the soldiers on the front line. I signed requisitions, wrote letters upon letters, and spent countless hours on the phone speaking with overbearing generals and impatient German government officials. Not a very glamorous job, was it? Anyway, that's what I did.'

'Well, the important thing is that you survived. When you think of all those soldiers who were killed, it makes me feel thankful that most Mexicans were not greatly affected.' She paused. 'It just occurred to me that you've never told me why you left Germany. You must miss your family and your friends.'

Hans cleared his throat. 'Yes, I do miss some of my friends. As for my family, well, the American bombs took care of that. It was just too sad for me to remain in Germany. Too many memories of the way things were before the war. But enough of the past, why don't we take a walk through the park? It's such a beautiful day.'

They walked to a fountain where a little boy dressed in a matching blue shirt and pants stood peering into the water.

'Look at all the money,' he said, excitedly, to his mother standing a few feet behind him.

Elena had a twinkle in her eye. She reached into her purse and pulled out a coin. She closed her eyes, then threw it into the fountain.

'What did you wish?' Hans asked.

'I can't tell you, otherwise it won't come true,' she said, smiling.

★　★　★

The dining room of the Gran Hotel was unusually quiet for a Friday night. Except for a lone diner who sat at the table next to them, they had the entire back of the restaurant to themselves.

Throughout the evening Elena barely touched her food as she sat mesmerized by Hans and his entertaining stories of his travels throughout Europe. She was in awe of him and listened intently until the waiter interrupted them.

'Will you be having dessert?' he asked, dutifully.

'No, thank you,' Hans said, without taking his eyes off Elena.

For a moment Hans became quiet, almost serious. After paying the bill, he got up and walked around the table to help her from her chair. She looked at him trustingly, and allowed him to escort her out of the dining room and up to his room.

★ ★ ★

'He was my life, and then he was gone,' she said, in a barely audible voice. 'I never saw him after that night.' She rose to her feet and made her way to the door. 'I have to go. Too much has happened and I need to be by myself.'

Antonio got up and followed her. 'You can't go out like this. Please, mother. Stay for a while. I know you're hurting and I want to help. It's not going to do any good to shut me out from your feelings, as painful as they may be.'

'I know you mean well, Antonio, but I'd rather sort out my feelings alone. Maybe tomorrow or the next day we can talk about it.' She gave him a gentle kiss on the cheek and quickly left the apartment.

15

Dressed in a nun's habit, Ivana walked past the information desk and made her way to the far wing on the other side of the courtyard. As she entered the corridor that led to Schumann's room, she saw an elderly priest and a young altar boy dressed in a white robe, walking in her direction. When they came within a couple of feet from each other, the priest nodded and said, 'Good afternoon, Sister.'

'Good afternoon, Father,' she said, without making eye contact.

They had just passed each other when the priest stopped and turned. 'Sister,' he said, calling out to her. 'I'll be celebrating Mass in the chapel in fifteen minutes. I don't wish to impose, but would you be so kind as to assist me?'

'Of course, Father,' she said, turning to him. 'I'll be there shortly.' She smiled politely and continued down the corridor. She stepped into the room, closed the door behind her and quietly walked up to Schumann who was sitting in his wheelchair, looking out the window. She pulled out a three-foot cord from the pocket of her coat and twirled it once around. Just as Schumann turned slightly to see who it was, she reached over his head and pulled the cord tightly around his neck. When he stopped breathing, she relaxed her muscles and removed the cord and replaced it with a red scarf that she tied into a noose. She stepped back for a moment, then quickly left the room. Moments later she stepped into a waiting car across the street from the nursing home.

'How did it go?' Rosenberg asked as he shifted into gear and slowly pulled away.

'Just like you said it would. I don't think he even knew what was happening to him.'

'That's too bad,' Rosenberg said. 'It's more than he deserved. But he's one less Nazi. That will show the rest of them that wherever they are, we'll get them sooner or later.'

★ ★ ★

Antonio was taking a shower when he heard the phone ring. He grabbed a terry cloth robe from a hook on the wall and rushed out to answer it.

It was Dr Pacheco.

'Have you read today's paper?' he asked.

'No, I just got up a few minutes ago. What is it?'

'Schumann is dead,' he blurted out. 'There's a small article about him on the fifth page of the main section. He was killed by some anti-Nazi group in Paraguay.'

With his hand, Antonio wiped off the beads of water over his eyes. 'Are you sure?' he said numbly. 'Maybe it's someone else.'

'I don't think so. Read the article for yourself, and if you want to talk about it you know where you can reach me. I just hope to God, your mother didn't see it.'

'If it's not on the front page, she probably didn't notice it,' Antonio said. 'She's not much for reading the paper.'

He hung up the phone and dashed out to pick up the newspaper from in front of his door. He quickly scanned the pages until he found the article:

MURDER OF EX-NAZI BLAMED ON EXTREMIST GROUP

An anti-Nazi group known as Jews for Justice or JFJ has claimed credit for the killing of Hans Schumann, a suspected Nazi war criminal who had lived in Paraguay for almost thirty years. Paralyzed and unable to speak, Schumann had been confined to Sanitorio El Paraiso in Asunción for the past eighteen months. According to local police officials, Schumann was found strangled with a red scarf tied around his neck. The red scarf is believed to be the trademark of an elusive and mysterious female assassin who in the past has killed other Nazi fugitives in a similar manner.

The newspaper still in his hand, Antonio walked back inside, and re-read the article. It was no coincidence. The red scarf, the lighter with the wrong initials. At the bar she had pretended to be out of matches. Very clever. A sudden chill went through his body as he realized how easily she had seduced him.

He looked for Pamela's phone number, found it under a pile of bills, and quickly dialled. She answered on the fourth ring.

'I was hoping to hear from you but I didn't think it would be this soon,' Pamela said. 'Is everything all right?'

'I guess you haven't heard.'

'Heard what?'

'My father is . . . dead. It came out in the paper this morning. The JFJ claimed credit for killing him.'

'Oh, my God!' she said. 'I'm the one who let them know where he was staying. I never thought they would kill him. It didn't make any sense. He was already half-dead. I feel terrible about it. I thought I was doing the

149

right thing. Antonio, I'm so sorry.'

'Don't be. I'm not exactly shedding any tears. Maybe in a few days I'll feel something. But what is there to feel? I met a stranger in a wheelchair, and now he's dead. I have to admit, though, I don't think I'll ever forget those intense, brown eyes that filled up with tears just moments after I stepped into the room.'

'What about your mother? Does she know?'

'I don't think so. It was a small article on the fifth page of the paper, so she probably missed it. It would tear her apart if she found out.'

'Did you tell her you had seen him in Paraguay?'

'Yes, but I didn't tell her about his physical condition. As it was, she took it pretty hard. I only hope that no one brings the article to her attention.'

Pamela sighed. 'I don't know what to say. As much as I wanted him dead, I never expected it would end this way. Rosenberg used me. I was so easily taken in by his rhetoric that I didn't see how dangerous he and his organization really were.'

'Look, it happened and there's nothing you or anyone can do about it. My only regret is that he and I never had a real conversation.

There are so many questions left unanswered, like whether or not he really loved my mother.' His voice started to break. 'I didn't mean to get heavy about this. I just wanted to let you know what happened.'

'I'm glad you called me,' she said, her voice dropping to almost a whisper. 'And thanks for not making me feel guilty.'

After a long silence, he said, 'I guess there's nothing more to say. It's really over, isn't it?'

★ ★ ★

Herman paced the floor in the basement where only days before he and Alfred had tried to talk to Antonio. Puffs of smoke from a fat cigar he was smoking followed him as he babbled about the old man's death.

'I just knew the son of a bitch was trouble,' he said. 'We should have killed him when we had the chance. We had him in this very room and we let him go. And that girl from Miami. She was up to no good. The two of them probably tipped off the JFJ and led them to him.'

'Sit down, Herman, I didn't come back here to get myself all worked up,' Alfred said. 'Let's look at this calmly. Maybe I'm wrong, but somehow I can't believe that Antonio would have deliberately led the JFJ to the old

151

man, knowing they were going to kill him.'

Herman shook his head. 'We were fooled by his face. The bastard only looked German. I'm telling you, we should have killed him. And the girl too. Who knows what he told her about us? We never should have let them leave the country.'

'As much as I hate to admit it, you may be right, Herman. But there's nothing we can do about it.' He leaned forward. 'Maybe this will work to our advantage.'

'What do you mean?' Herman asked.

'Well, now that the old man is dead, I hardly think Antonio will have any desire to come here again. As long as the old man was alive, Antonio always had a reason to come back either alone or with others. In a way, the JFJ did us a favor.'

'Some favor,' Herman said. 'The poor man didn't deserve to die the way he did.'

'No, but let's face it. He was never going to get better. At least he no longer has to live through the indignity of being little more than a human vegetable.'

Herman flicked the ashes from his cigar. 'When you put it that way . . . '

'In any case,' Alfred said sharply. 'We're not going to allow this to happen again. When I return to Buenos Aires, I'm going to call for a special session to propose that we put up a sizeable bounty for the assassin's head.'

* * *

Antonio had just hung up with Pamela when the phone rang and he picked it up on the first ring.

It was Dr Pacheco.

'I'm with your mother,' he said. 'I just wanted you to know she's very upset and — '

'What happened?'

'She found out about your father. She saw a TV newscast. After she called me, I got here as fast I could. She's taking it very hard.'

'I was afraid of this,' Antonio said. 'I'll be there in ten minutes.'

'No . . . wait. There's really no need for you to come here, at least not for a while.'

'Nonsense, she's my mother and she needs me. Tell her I'll be there as fast as I can.' He hung up the phone and dashed out the door.

* * *

From across the room, Antonio saw his mother sitting at the dining table with her head resting on her arms crossed over. Sitting next to her was Dr Pacheco, who immediately stood up and placed a protective hand on her shoulder.

'I'm so sorry, mother,' Antonio said as he walked towards her. 'I was hoping you would never have to hear about it.'

His mother sobbed inconsolably.

'Is there anything I can do?' Antonio asked. 'Maybe if we talk about it or if you just want me to listen, that's fine too. I know you're hurting and I want to help. It's no good to keep it all inside.'

She slowly raised her head and looked at him. 'You don't understand, Antonio, and I don't expect you to. There's nothing you can do for me. I've got to work this out by myself. I just want to be alone. If you love me, please let me be alone.'

Dr Pacheco gestured to Antonio to walk with him to the other end of the room.

'Maybe it's best to do as she asks,' he whispered. 'It's part of the grieving process to want to be alone. When she's ready to talk, she'll let you know. But don't try to press her. Just coming here to show her you care is enough for now. Believe me, I know what I'm talking about.'

'I respect your opinion, Doctor Pacheco, but I can't just walk away. Look at her, she's falling apart.'

'Look, Antonio, I didn't want to say this,

but part of what your mother finds difficult to cope with is . . . well, the fact that you look so much like your father. Don't you see, every time she looks at you, she sees him, and it hurts her, especially now that he's gone forever.'

Antonio took a moment to digest what Dr Pacheco had said. 'I just can't believe it,' he said, finally. 'I'm beginning to think that my face is a curse. With other people it didn't matter, but with my own mother, it's just too much.' He shook his head. 'I'd better get going.'

16

Throughout the morning Antonio had resisted picking up the phone to call his mother. Had he given her enough time? Impulsively, he picked up the phone and dialled her number. He let it ring seven times, then hung up. It was almost a relief that she didn't answer.

He went back to reviewing his mail and picked up an envelope marked personal and confidential, with no return address. The postmark on the top right corner revealed it had been mailed from Berlin just two days before he had left for El Paso. Maybe it was something from Bergman, he thought, as he tore open the envelope and pulled out a handwritten letter.

You're probably wondering why a stranger from Germany is writing to you. Permit me to explain. I recently found out through certain people whose names are not important, that you had discovered that Hans Schumann is your father. By now you have probably been told he was responsible for committing certain crimes during the war. I can only guess what you must think of these allegations, and for that reason, I am asking you to consider that you are getting only one side of the story.

And what is the other side, you might ask? Well, first I'll have to begin by telling you something about myself. Prior to the war, I was a history professor at the university of Berlin. When the war broke out, many of my colleagues who were Jewish, or had even a drop of Jewish blood dating back to their great grandparents, were immediately arrested by the SS. Their plight did not concern me or directly affect me. That is, not until a young SS officer came to my office one morning and informed me that the SS had received information that my deceased mother was Jewish. I was stunned and refused to believe it. We talked — at least I talked — and he listened patiently, if not sympathetically. Incredibly, he told me he would postpone my arrest. For how long, he could not say.

I'm sure you've guessed by now that the young officer was your father, Hans Schumann. He is a remarkable man to whom I will forever be indebted.

Now, I'm an old man and time is running out. And so writing to you is the *very least I can do for your father. Please do not be so quick to judge him. There is a good and benevolent side to your father and I hope you will not be swayed by those who are only interested in vengeance and retribution.*

A grateful friend

Antonio placed the letter on the table and stared at it for a long moment. It had affected him in a way that he didn't think was possible. Maybe his father wasn't the monster that everyone had portrayed him to be. Maybe reports about him had been exaggerated. Maybe someone else was responsible for the things he was alleged to have done. Maybe . . . he stopped in mid-thought and placed the letter back in the envelope. His father was dead. It really didn't matter whether he had a good and benevolent side as the letter suggested, or whether or not the JFJ was justified in killing him. Nothing could change the fact that his father had deceived and abandoned his mother.

His secretary's voice startled him over the intercom. 'Señor de la Vega, I know you told me to hold your calls, but Señor Dominguez is on the phone. He sounds very irritated. He's asking about the contract for the construction project that you were supposed to have for him today. Do you want to speak to him?'

'No, just tell him that . . . that the contract will be ready for him to sign by noon tomorrow.' He'd have to hustle to get it ready by then, he thought, searching for the project folder among a stack of folders. It wasn't there. He suddenly remembered he had left it at home where he had intended to work on it before his life had turned into a living nightmare.

He stood up, put on his coat, and walked out of his office. 'I'll be back in a few minutes,' he said to his secretary. 'If my mother should call, tell her I'll call her back as soon as I return.'

★ ★ ★

Antonio entered his apartment and went straight to his bedroom. He paused in mid-step as he looked across the room and saw his desk area in disarray. The drawers were pulled open and there were papers strewn all over the floor. 'Burglars' flashed through his mind. He cautiously went throughout the entire apartment and found nothing missing. There was an expensive stereo, a few pieces of gold jewellery, a couple of antique vases, and even some cash he had left on the night stand. It didn't make any sense. He returned to his bedroom and sat on the bed.

He was about to pick up the money when he noticed the picture of his father that had been sitting on the night stand was gone. His entire body suddenly tensed up. Flashbacks of Alfred and Herman immediately entered his brain. They couldn't seriously believe he was still a threat to them. They had gone too far, and he wasn't about to wait for them to try something else. He grabbed the phone, dialled the operator and asked for the federal police. While he waited on hold, his eye caught the tip end of a red scarf that had been stuffed under a pillow. He hung up the phone and reached to pull it.

Holding the scarf in his hand, he whispered her name. 'Ivana.' He could feel his neck muscles tighten. She had left it as her calling card. But why? What did she want from him?

He got up, went to his desk, and pulled out the project folder. After checking around the room once more, he left his apartment and headed back to his office. Throughout the short walk, he had the uneasy feeling he was being watched.

★ ★ ★

'Have any strangers come into the office the past couple of days?' Antonio asked his secretary. 'Like an attractive woman with an unusual accent?'

She shook her head. 'Not that I recall. But there were those phone calls?'

'What phone calls?'

'I left the messages on your desk along with your mail. I assumed you looked them over.'

He dashed into his office and quickly went through his messages. There were two strangely worded messages left by a woman caller who didn't leave a name.

The first one said: *You're too clever for your own good. Don't play games with us.* The second one said: *Don't look now, but someone is watching you.*

He crumpled the messages in his hand and tossed them into the waste basket. He had to get out of there and go someplace where he could figure out what was going on.

'I'll be at the Hotel de Cortez, Maria,' he said on the way out. 'Don't expect me back for at least a couple of hours.'

★ ★ ★

The head waiter immediately recognized him and rushed to greet him. 'Señor de la Vega, it's good to see you,' he said warmly. 'We've missed you these past few days.'

'Thank you, Pedro. It's good to be back.' He looked around the courtyard and spotted a few familiar faces. It made him feel safe.

'Will you be having your usual glass of sherry?' the waiter asked, following him to his table.

'Yes, make sure it's cold.'

'We have an excellent special today,' the waiter said. 'Extra large shrimp in a light garlic sauce with cilantro rice.'

'That'll be fine,' Antonio said, not wanting to look over the menu.

'Very good. I'll be back with your sherry.'

Antonio unconsciously played with his silverware as he thought about Ivana and her friends. There was no telling when or where they would show up next. Her message that he was being watched clicked in his mind as he spotted a European-looking man in his mid-thirties sitting alone at a table toward the rear of the patio. The man appeared nervous and kept looking around. Occasionally, he would glance in Antonio's direction. Seconds later, a young, heavy-set woman and a little girl just barely old enough to walk, joined him and the man quickly signalled the waiter. Antonio gave out a sigh of relief. He was beginning to suspect anyone who looked different or out of place. But until he learned

162

what Ivana and her friends were after, he wasn't going to take any chances.

He didn't notice her as she walked up from behind and softly said, 'Hello, Antonio.'

He turned around. 'Pamela,' he said, rising to his feet. 'What are you doing here? I hope you didn't come because of my phone call.'

She had the same serious expression as when she first knocked on his hotel room door in Asunción.

'As a matter of fact, your phone call has a lot to do with my being here,' she said.

'Please, have a seat,' he said. He pulled out a chair for her and signalled the waiter to bring her a glass of wine. 'It must be something really important, at least enough to bring you here so unexpectedly.'

She placed her purse on the chair next to her. 'After I got home,' she began slowly, 'I did a lot of crying. I just couldn't stop myself. I would look at my father's picture on the bureau and I would talk to him as if he were still alive. I wanted him to know that what he had started was over. But then when I discovered that it wasn't really over, I freaked out. I didn't know what to do so I packed my bags and decided to tell you in person.'

'Tell me what?' he said, a curiously.

Pamela hesitated. 'Your father is still alive.'

'What are you saying?' he asked incredulously. 'My father is dead. I read about it in the newspaper. It even came out on television.'

'I'm telling you he's still alive,' she insisted.

'You're not making any sense, Pamela. Are you saying that the story about his murder by the JFJ is not true?'

'No, that's not what I'm trying to say,' she said shaking her head. 'Don't you see what's happened? That old man we went to see was not your father. They killed the wrong man and I'm responsible for that.'

'But why are you so sure he wasn't my father? You didn't go in to see him. I did. And I'm telling you, he was definitely my father. He had my features and — '

'What color were his eyes?'

'They were brown. But what does that have to do with anything?'

'Schumann's eyes were blue. The man you met was someone else. After your phone call when you talked about his brown eyes filling up with tears, I had a sense that something was not right. I wasn't really sure what it was, and then it suddenly hit me. In his diary, my father had written about his nightmares. *His cold, blue eyes devoid of any emotion look straight at me just moments before he pulls the trigger.* Those were his exact words.'

164

'I . . . I don't know what to say,' Antonio stammered. 'I'm not sure whether I'm glad or angry that my father is still alive.' He clenched his jaw. 'They were very clever, weren't they? Those bastards figured I wouldn't get past seeing a paralyzed old man in a wheelchair. They almost got away with it. And they would have, if it hadn't been for you.'

The waiter placed their drinks on the table. 'Would the señorita like to see a menu?' he asked.

'No,' Antonio said, before she had a chance to answer. 'And if it's not too late, tell the chef to hold the shrimp. I've suddenly lost my appetite.'

'I'm sorry, Antonio,' Pamela said. 'I know what you must be thinking. And I can understand how much simpler it would be if it really had been your father who died in that nursing home. But now the question is, what are you going to do?'

'What do you mean?'

'I'm asking if you still feel the same as when we were in Paraguay?'

'Look, Pamela, nothing has changed. I admit that I've had some mixed feelings about him, but I can assure you I have no sympathy for this man. He's my biological father and that's all he is to me. Just as you

165

can't erase what he did to your father and his family, I can't forget what he did to my mother.'

'I'm glad to hear that because I'm determined to resume the search to find him and I was hoping you'd join me.'

'It's not going to be that easy, you know. But like I said, nothing has changed. I still want to meet him, face to face.'

'Good,' she said with a trace of a smile. 'We'll put our heads together and pick up where we left off.'

They raised their glasses slightly.

'By the way,' Pamela said. 'I called Bergman right before I left for the airport. I wanted him to know that I felt certain your father was still alive. I told him I was on my way to see you and possibly make plans to return to Paraguay. He wanted me to keep him advised and I promised I would.'

'Well, at least one mystery is solved,' Antonio said.

'What's that?'

Antonio took a sip of his sherry. 'Ivana. We saw her getting into the elevator in the hotel the night you arrived. She and her friends are in town. They've apparently figured out that the man they killed was not my father. They broke into my apartment this morning while I was at the office. I guess they think I'm in contact with him. Can you believe that?'

'You obviously know more about this woman than I do. Are you sure it was her?'

'Positive. She left something behind to let me know it was her.'

'What was it?'

'A red scarf. She's got this thing about red scarves. It's hard to explain. It even came out in the newspaper that the man who was killed was found with a red scarf tied around his neck.'

Pamela sighed. 'It looks like I really made a mess of things. If I hadn't called Rosenberg after we got back from the nursing home, the old man would still be alive today, and maybe Ivana wouldn't be here trying to check up on you.'

'You thought you were doing the right thing,' he said, trying to make her feel better. 'What's done is done. When you think about it, they fell for the deception just like we did.'

'Thanks for being so understanding. It's just a shame that we're having to go through this again after we thought it was all behind us.'

'Well, before we do anything, we need to make sure we can leave without being noticed. We can't afford to let Ivana and her cohorts know what we're up to. I just hope they don't know you're in town. If they see

167

you, they may assume you're here for the same reason they are. Where are you staying?'

'The Aristos Hotel.'

'Good, you'll blend in with all the tourists from the Zona Rosa.'

She reached for her glass. 'So what's our next step?'

'I'm not really sure. But first I have to figure out what I'm going to tell my mother. She took it pretty hard when she saw a TV news bulletin about the old man's death. It sent her into a very deep depression and I'm worried about her. But thank God for Doctor Pacheco.'

'Who's Doctor Pacheco?'

'He's an old friend of the family and he's been very good to her. I know he'll continue to be there for her. Right now, he's the only one she'll speak to. I'm afraid I haven't been much help to her. Something to do with my face. Doctor Pacheco thinks that I remind her too much of my father.'

'Why don't you just tell her that he's not dead?' she said. 'If she's as depressed as you say she is, it can only help.'

'But for how long? A month? A year? If I tell her the truth, all I'll be doing is buying some extra time. When we find him — and I'm determined that we will — it may be the same thing all over again. I'll have to think about it. Right now, I need to get back to my office to take care of some things. If we're going to be away for a few days, I want to make sure my secretary will be able to cover for me.'

'Before you go . . . I want you to take this with you,' she said hesitantly. She reached into her purse, pulled out a video cassette and handed it to Antonio.

'What's this?'

'There's a Holocaust research center in Miami that video records interviews with victims of the Holocaust. After I realized that Schumann was still alive, I went to the center on the off-chance that someone would recognize his name. To my surprise, the director of the center told me that an old Polish woman had only recently appeared to tell her story of the Nazi who had brutalized her and her sister.'

'I don't think I need to see proof that my father was a cold-blooded killer,' Antonio said defensively.

'Take it anyway. You don't have to tell me if you see it. I just want to make sure that if and when we find your father, you won't have any second thoughts about turning him in.'

Antonio didn't say anything as he stood up, and then quietly walked away.

17

In his apartment, Antonio poured himself a glass of brandy and stared at the video cassette sitting on top of the coffee table. He wished Pamela hadn't given it to him. After a few moments, he picked up the cassette, walked over to the VCR and popped it in the machine. He felt an all-too-familiar knot in his stomach as he pressed the play button and sat back to view it.

The old woman looked fit and healthy for her age and spoke with only a trace of an accent. She seemed remarkably controlled as she began to relate the details of her story.

'I was nineteen years old and my sister was sixteen when we arrived at the camp. The long ride on the cattle car had been very hard on her and she could barely walk. After we were stripped of our clothing and our dignity we were assigned to a barracks where we thought we would be able to get some rest. But it was not to be.

'The young SS officer in charge ordered everyone out of the barracks. He wanted to personally inspect each one of us as we stood in formation for a long time. By the time he got to me and my sister, she was ready to collapse and, in fact, she did. As she tried to get up, she began to spit up blood and some of it spilled onto the SS officer's boots. He became enraged and yelled obscenities at her, and then he began to beat her viciously with a riding crop he carried with him. I instinctively rushed to protect her, and he turned the crop on me and beat me, over and over. When he was through we managed to drag ourselves back into the barracks and we finally were able to sleep for a few hours.

'When morning came I got up to check on my sister. 'Hilda, wake up, wake up,' I said to her. I reached for her hand — it was cold — and I squeezed it gently. 'Please, Hilda, open your eyes and look at me,' I said with tears in my eyes. I tried shaking her and calling out her name again, but it was no use. She had slipped away from us in the middle of the night. My poor, lovely sister, who had dreams of being a concert pianist, was dead because a few drops of her blood had stained the polished boots of a Nazi officer.'

The old woman paused to wipe away the tears from her eyes and apologized for the interruption. 'I'm sorry,' she said. 'But it's hard for me to speak about this. I loved her so much and there was nothing I could do to save her.'

'We understand,' said a sympathetic voice in the background. 'Just take as much time as you need.'

'I'm all right,' she responded. 'I'd like to continue. It's very important to me that you record what I have to say because it's the least I can do for my sister. History and the rest of the world should know that what happened during that period of time was real, and it could happen again.'

'Missus Goldman, can you tell us something about the SS officer who beat you and your sister?' the voice in the background inquired. 'Do you know his name or what he looked like?'

'A few days after my sister died, I learned that his name was Hans Schumann. He was transferred out of the camp shortly afterwards, but I'll never forget his face. He had piercing blue eyes, light brown hair, and he looked very German. I mean he had features that one would consider German. He was also very tall and thin. If I saw him today I know I could recognize him. I am old and he is old, but there's something about the eyes that never changes. I would recognize him by his eyes. My biggest hope before I die is to see him arrested and brought to justice.'

The tape abruptly ended and Antonio just sat there for several moments, staring blankly

172

at the screen. For the rest of the evening, he wept intermittently and tried to come to terms with the fact that his father was, indeed, the monster that the Polish woman and others had portrayed him to be.

* * *

Pamela heard a knock at the door and rushed to answer it. She was expecting room service and didn't bother to look through the viewer.

'You might as well come in,' she said when she saw who it was. 'We have a lot to talk about.'

'Yes, we do,' Rosenberg said, glumly. He stepped into the room and took a seat on the edge of the bed.

She pulled up a chair and sat across from him.

'I know why you're here,' she said. 'But before we get into that, I want you to know that I feel betrayed and partly to blame for the murder of that man in Paraguay. He was old and sick. In his condition he probably didn't have very long to live.' She paused to collect herself. 'You killed a totally innocent man and there's nothing I can do about it because I was part of it. May God forgive me.'

'I'm glad you realize that it was you who

tipped us off,' Rosenberg said. 'The authorities would probably find it difficult to believe that you did it for any other reason than to assist our organization. But why dwell on the negative? The old man was probably a Nazi criminal like Schumann. I'm certainly not going to shed any tears for him. Besides, it was Schumann's friends who created the deception in the first place. So, if you want to blame someone, blame them. My advice is to forget about it.'

'I can't believe you're being so cavalier about it,' she said. 'What you and your friends did was as cold-blooded as anything the Nazis ever did. I almost feel sorry for you because somehow you've lost your ability to feel for people. The poor man you killed was a human being and there's nothing you can say that will justify what you did.'

'Look, the old man is dead and buried. I admit that maybe we should've held off doing anything until we checked him out. But the fact is, we didn't and regardless of how it happened, we still have a mission to carry out, which is the reason I came to see you.'

'If you think I'm going to help you ever again, you're very much mistaken. And you can forget about trying to appeal to my Jewish conscience. It won't work. Not this time.'

'I'm sorry you feel that way. At least I know where you stand. But what about Antonio?'

'What about him?'

'Well, we think he was in on the deception from the very beginning. Like I told you before, people like him do not go against their own kind. We believe he's in contact with his father, and as far as we're concerned, that makes him just as much a target.'

She shook her head. 'I can't believe what I'm hearing,' she said, her voice rising. 'You and your friends are not only unfeeling, but you also are not very smart. I just left Antonio a few hours ago and he doesn't know where his father is any more than I do. I think I know him a little better than you do and I can assure you he has absolutely no feelings for his father.'

Rosenberg stroked his chin and gave her a sceptical look. 'I think you're a little naïve about these things,' he said. 'For your sake I hope he doesn't let you down. Remember what I said about the blood. All you have to do is look at his German face. It's the identification factor. He may not even be aware of it, but it's there, nonetheless.'

'You make it sound as if it's all genetics. But you're wrong and the proof will be when we see Schumann brought to trial and legally made to pay for his crimes.'

Rosenberg abruptly stood up. 'We'll just have to wait and see, won't we?'

Pamela remained seated and waited for him to leave.

'By the way,' he said, opening the door. 'I hope you're not falling in love with him. That would be a big mistake.' He closed the door and left Pamela wondering why he had said that.

She got up, picked up the phone and dialled Antonio's number. She let it ring six times, hung up and dialled it again.

'I was just about to hang up,' she said, when he finally answered. 'I wanted to let you know that Rosenberg was just here. It's really incredible. After what he and his friends did to that man in Paraguay, he had the nerve to show his face.'

'He must have followed you after you left the restaurant. I kind of had a feeling we were being watched. What did he want?'

'He wanted to know if you had been in contact with your father. Of course, I told him that you didn't have any more information about him than I did.'

'Did he believe you?'

'I'm not sure. Unbelievably, he tried to convince me that . . . that you — '

'What? It's my face again, isn't it? Everyone assumes that my German features are directly tied to the way I think, the way I feel. Well, Rosenberg's wrong and I'm going to prove it by finding my father and personally seeing to it that he pays for his crimes.'

'Hey, take it easy,' she said. 'I know it upsets you but you can't let it get to you. What a man like Rosenberg thinks doesn't really matter. In a way it's probably good that he came to see me because now it's all out in the open and everyone knows where we stand. I let him know that you and I are a team.'

'Thanks for the vote of confidence,' he said, his voice a little calmer. 'I kind of needed that tonight.'

By the sound of his voice Pamela knew he had seen the video.

18

The SS officer pointed his Luger at the back of the head of a frightened Jewish man standing on the edge of a cliff. Suddenly the gun fired and the man fell over the cliff. Antonio screamed in the darkness and sat up and shook his head to make sure the nightmare had left.

★ ★ ★

'My advice is that you tell her the truth,' Dr Pacheco said, sitting in his study across from Antonio.

'But won't it make it worse?' Antonio asked. 'The last thing I want to do is add to her misery. I'm just not convinced that telling her that my father is alive is the right thing to do. Right now she thinks he's dead and she's trying to cope with it. Eventually she'll have to accept it.'

'A few days ago I might have agreed with you. But after spending a lot of time talking and listening to your mother, I think she deserves to know the truth. Don't you see that by telling her that he really didn't die in that nursing home, we're giving her something to cling to, something to make it easier for her to remember him as he was.'

Antonio slowly rose to his feet. 'Very well, if you think it's best. I only hope that I'm doing the right thing.'

Dr Pacheco nodded and stood up to see him to the door. 'Please trust me on this,' he said. 'Just don't blurt it out. You'll know how best to tell her.'

'Before I go . . . I need to ask your opinion about something. It has to do with a nightmare I had last night.'

Dr Pacheco looked at him curiously. 'What kind of nightmare?'

'It's about . . . an SS officer who shoots someone,' he said hesitantly. 'He points a pistol to the back of this Jewish man standing on the edge of a cliff, and then he pulls the trigger, and the man falls over the cliff.'

'What else happened?' Dr Pacheco asked sympathetically.

'That's it. I suddenly woke up and it was over.'

'It seems to me that what you dreamed is very normal considering what you know about your father and the horrible crimes he committed. It probably wouldn't be a bad idea to take a few days off just to do nothing, or at least nothing that has to do with your father and all that business.'

'But you don't understand. In the dream I'm the SS officer who shoots the Jewish man.'

There was a long silence. 'Well, it doesn't mean anything and you shouldn't focus on it,' Dr Pacheco said. 'My recommendation is still the same. What you need is a few days away from all of this.'

'Didn't you hear what I said? I'm the one doing the shooting!'

'Look, Antonio. Take my advice and don't try to make anything out of this dream of yours. Even the experts can't agree on these things.'

★　★　★

Ivana was sitting on the couch with her legs slightly open, oblivious to the fact Rosenberg could see a good portion of her thighs all the way up to her crotch. 'So are we just going to hang around this place indefinitely — waiting for something to happen?' she said.

'Look, I don't like being here any more than you do,' Rosenberg said. 'But we have no choice. Even if Pamela was right about Antonio, sooner or later they're going to try to make contact with Schumann. And when they do, we'll be close by and this time, there

180

will be no mistakes. By the way, too many people saw you in Asunción and they may recognize you. So I would advise that you change your appearance.'

'Don't tell me what to do,' she said. 'I'm a professional and I know what I have to do. Just worry about yourself and don't fuck it up like you did the last time.'

'I told you it wasn't my fault,' he said defensively. 'It wasn't anybody's fault. When Pamela told me she and Antonio had just seen him at the nursing home I — '

'You just blindly assumed it was him without checking it out. But never mind about that. What we've got to do is make sure we stay close to Antonio. Do you have enough men?'

'Yes, I brought them in especially for this. Most of them lost entire families during the Holocaust and they're committed to staying with us for as long as necessary.'

*   *   *

The knife made a dull whacking sound as it cut off the top of a large carrot.

'So what is so important?' Antonio's mother asked, her hand wrapped around the knife's handle. She purposely avoided looking at him and continued to cut the

181

carrot into small slices.

'Can you please stop what you're doing and listen to me,' Antonio said, standing off to one side.

She ignored him and picked up another carrot and began to cut into it.

'Mother, I know how upset you are. But please listen to me. I just spoke to Doctor Pacheco and he thought — '

'I would appreciate it if you would stop talking to Doctor Pacheco behind my back,' she said, her voice edgy. 'I'm perfectly capable of taking care of myself and I don't need you to constantly seek Doctor Pacheco's advice about things that have nothing to do with you. It's my problem and I'll deal with it alone. I'm sure you mean well, but please just go about your business and leave me to mine.'

She reached for a small onion and began to peel it layer by layer.

'What I came here to tell you is that there's been a mistake about my father. It seems that it was somebody else who was killed in that nursing home. That means . . . he's alive, mother.'

She stopped peeling the onion and her eyes quickly filled with tears.

'Peeling onions always makes me cry,' she said, stoically.

Antonio quietly left her to assimilate the news in her own way. He felt an uneasy gnawing in the pit of his stomach and hoped to God he had done the right thing.

★ ★ ★

From their table at the terrace restaurant on the roof of the Majestic Hotel, Antonio and Pamela had a perfect view of the heart of the old city. They saw locals and tourists alike walking along a large, open square called the Zocalo. To the left they saw faithful worshippers, mostly old women, meandering in and out of the nearly 500-year-old Metropolitan Cathedral. And they saw the ever-present Indian women sitting outside the gates to the cathedral, selling their hand-made crafts and candy.

'I'm glad you suggested this place,' Pamela said, her eyes focused on the ruins of the great Aztec temple to the right of the cathedral. 'It's magnificent. I'm only sorry I didn't accompany my parents on their vacation. Mother had asked me to come, but I was too busy. It probably would have been a good opportunity to spend some time with them, especially with my father.' She smiled wistfully. 'I wish I were here under different circumstances. There's so

183

much to see and do.'

'Now that you mention it, I hope that some day when this is all behind us, you'll come back, strictly as a tourist. I'd like nothing better than to show you my city. Of course, it will take at least a couple of weeks to see everything that's worth seeing.'

'That sounds like an invitation,' she said with a quick smile.

'It is. I mean it. I don't know how all of this is going to end, but I'd like to think that it won't affect our friendship.'

She looked away for a moment. 'I'll be honest with you. I really don't know how I'll feel when this is all over. I guess I still see us wanting to do what's right but for different reasons.' She picked up a glass of water and took a drink. 'Let's walk through the Zocalo. Do you mind?'

'No, it's a good idea. We can talk as we walk.'

She excused herself to freshen up in the ladies room while Antonio paid the bill.

★ ★ ★

They made a quick dash across the busy street and slowly began to walk in the direction of the National Palace on the other side of the Zocalo.

184

'I was thinking that maybe we should wait before going back to Paraguay,' he said. 'As long as Rosenberg and his friends are convinced that we're probably going back to look for my father, they're going to hang around and keep an eye on us.'

'I think you're right. Rosenberg's visit to my room last night was just an indication of how serious he is about getting to Schumann through any means he can. I seriously doubt that after he left the room he just packed up and left the city. But how long should we wait?'

'I don't know,' Antonio said. 'We'll just have to take it one day at a time until we feel it's safe to go.'

'But that may take a week or longer.'

'I know. That's why I think you should go back to Miami and wait until you hear from me. They can't keep watching us forever.'

'I guess we have no choice,' she said, disappointed. 'But how will you know when it's safe?'

'Just be ready to travel at a moment's notice. It would probably be better if you fly directly from Miami to Paraguay and I'll just meet you there.'

★　★　★

185

Standing behind a news stand just across the Zocalo, a stocky man with east European features kept a watchful eye on the couple. He wore a small Star of David around his neck, and had a nervous habit of pulling on it with his thumb and forefinger.

★ ★ ★

'Incidentally, I told my mother that my father was alive,' Antonio said. 'Doctor Pacheco convinced me that it was the best thing to do.'

'I really feel for her,' Pamela said. 'She's an innocent victim and I wish there was a way to spare her from all of this. I'd like to meet her some day.'

'She'd like you, I'm sure. But I'm afraid it'll be a while before she feels comfortable meeting new people. Even I haven't been all that welcome around her, lately.'

'I'm sure that'll pass. Just be patient with her.'

They walked past the palace to the corner of the Zocala, then slowly made a diagonal turn in the opposite direction toward the cathedral. Just ahead of them a little Indian girl and her mother sat on the hard surface in front of a row of hand-made dolls. They were cute little dolls dressed in colorful outfits, some with a single braid down their back and others with two braids hanging freely. As Antonio and Pamela came within a couple of feet from where they were sitting, the little Indian girl picked up a doll and held it out for Pamela to take it.

'*No, gracias*,' Pamela said, shaking her head. The girl gave up easily and turned to her mother, who said something to her in their native dialect. She handed the little girl a different doll, one with a bright red apron, and urged her to give it another try. Holding the doll in her hand, the little girl stood up and ran up to Pamela to show her the doll. Unlike the smiling face on the doll, the little girl had a sad look in her eyes that struck Pamela's heart.

Pamela took the doll from the little girl and paid her a few pesos. Without saying a word, the little girl ran back to her mother and handed her the money.

'I think there's an afternoon flight to Miami,' Pamela said unexpectedly. 'I might as well check out of my hotel and try to make it.'

'What's the hurry? I thought we might have dinner tonight and go over some ideas about what we're going to do in Paraguay.'

'To be honest, it makes me feel uncomfortable to think that Rosenberg and his friends may be lurking around. The sooner they know I've gone back to Miami, the sooner they may decide to back off and leave town.'

'Maybe you're right,' he said, a hint of disappointment in his voice. 'I'll get you a cab.'

★ ★ ★

'We're living in the past because that is all we have left,' Alfred said, pointing to the plaques and pictures on a wall of the room where weeks before they had met to discuss Friedman and his letter to Bergman. 'I, for one, am not prepared to suffer the humiliation of seeing our names and the names of other good Germans dragged through the mud. And that is exactly what will happen if we allow another former SS officer to go through a public trial. But that is not the worst of it. We are all too familiar with the anti-Nazi fervour that follows such trials. Don't you see, it's not just our dignity, or what's left of it, that we stand to lose. It's our very existence.'

'I think you're making too much of it,' Alexander said, crushing his cigarette in a pewter ashtray. 'Schumann was overly upset when he said what he did. He was very close to his brother, and he blames himself for his death.'

'I agree with Alexander,' Josef said. 'No one

was more loyal to the Führer than he. We should give him the benefit of a doubt and try to help him overcome his grief. I, personally, fought alongside him in Poland and I know he would never do something so crazy as to return to Germany.'

Alfred crossed his arms. 'Both of you may be right,' he said. 'But we can't ignore what Herman has reported. Just this morning, I spoke to him, and he said that Schumann is still in a very serious state of depression. He won't listen to anyone. Even his closest friends can't seem to help him.'

'He's grieving for his brother and he's saying things he really doesn't mean,' Alexander said. 'All of us have lost a loved one and we all handle it differently. So maybe this is just his way of coping with what's happened.'

'Obviously, you think we should do something, Alfred,' Josef said. 'But there really isn't anything to do, is there? He's confused and he's got it into his head that he wants to go back to Germany even if it means certain death for him. Just give it some time and the problem will resolve itself.'

'It's not that simple,' Alfred said. 'We must be ready to act if the problem, as you put it, doesn't resolve itself. Herman is more than a little concerned about him and wants to know what we, as the head council, intend to do about it.'

'All right,' Alexander said. 'We know where this is leading. So let's put everything on the table. I say we keep a very close watch on him. We'll tell Herman to assign someone to stay close to him. Day and night, if necessary, until he comes to his senses.'

Alfred shook his head. 'We've got to face the possibility that he may never get this crazy idea out of his head. We've got to have some kind of plan to make sure that if he ever does something to threaten our security, we'll be ready to do what is necessary.'

'Speaking as his friend, I hope it never comes to that,' Alexander said.

'We all hope it never will,' Alfred said. 'But like it or not, we must be ready to act. If we're all in agreement, I'll notify Herman and tell him that we've come to a decision.'

★ ★ ★

When the phone rang, Antonio looked at his watch. It was almost midnight. He took his time getting up from the couch to answer it.

'Sorry to call you so late,' Dr Pacheco said. 'But I just left your mother and I thought you'd want to know she's doing much better.'

190

'Thank God,' Antonio said. 'When I left her this morning, I didn't know whether I had done the right thing.'

'Well, you did. Just knowing that your father is alive has made all the difference. It's hard to explain but she's beginning to sound like her old self.'

'You can't imagine how glad I am to hear that, Doctor Pacheco. Ever since I returned from Paraguay, there's been a wall between us and maybe now she and I can sit down and talk like we used to.'

'I'm glad you said that because that's one of the reasons I'm calling. Your mother seems to have regained her sense of hope. Call it false hope, if you like, but at her stage in life, that's all that she has. That's why I'm asking you not to take it away from her.'

'I wouldn't do anything to hurt her, you know that.'

'Well then, I'm asking you as an old friend who cares for your mother as much as you do, to give up this quest for your father and let it all stay in the past where it belongs. For her sake don't go out and do something that you'll regret.'

'I wish it were that simple. Too much has happened since I first learned he existed. I'm sorry, Doctor Pacheco, but I have to finish what I set out to do. I love my mother very much and I'll do my very best to protect her.'

'I hope you do, Antonio, and I hope you'll think about what I said.'

19

Wearing a dark blue, pin-striped suit Antonio looked out of place as he sat on the bench in the middle of Alameda Park waiting for his mother to appear. Her unexpected phone call had left him wondering what she was up to and why she had chosen to meet in the same place she used to meet his father.

'There you are,' he said, standing up to greet her and kiss her on the cheek.

Antonio couldn't help but notice a glow in her face. She seemed anxious to tell him something.

'I've done a lot of thinking,' she said as they sat down to talk. 'Especially since you told me that your father was still alive.'

'I know it hasn't been easy for you — '

'Please let me finish, Antonio. I've got a lot to say and I want you to listen. I asked you to meet me here because this park, this bench, they hold a lot of memories for me. I've kept them to myself, secretly hoping, praying that some day Hans would return.' She paused and looked across the park. 'I haven't been here since the last time he and I met here. I used to love this park, but I just couldn't deal with the rush of memories, so I just stayed away all these years.'

'I'm not sure I understand, mother. If this place makes you uncomfortable, why did you want to meet here?'

There was a brief silence. 'I've made an important decision. After you left yesterday morning, I broke down and cried. Just to know he was alive suddenly renewed my hopes and dreams. I couldn't do anything the rest of the day. Doctor Pacheco dropped by later and we talked for a while. He's such a good friend. I don't know what I would have done without him all these years. After he left, I realized that something was wrong. I had spent more than half my life living a sad, empty existence. I had cheated myself from leading a normal life and I cheated you, too, because you deserved a better, happier mother.'

'You were always there for me, mother,' Antonio said reassuringly. 'I never wanted for anything.'

'Let me continue. What I'm trying to say is that I've decided it's time to let go of the past. Knowing that your father is alive has made it easier for me to make that decision. I still love him and I always will. But I must go forward and make new plans, new friends. Maybe even take a long vacation.'

'I . . . I don't know what to say. This is totally unexpected. Have you told Doctor Pacheco?'

'No, I wanted to tell you first. You can't imagine how much better I feel just being able to talk about it with you. All those secrets, all those painful memories are behind me and I don't want them to control me ever again.'

She paused, then reached into her purse and pulled out an unusual-looking coin.

'Your father gave this to me the last time I saw him,' she said holding it in her hand. 'He told me it meant a great deal to him and he wanted me to have it as a keepsake. From that day on, I was never without it. Over the years it became a kind of symbol of the love we shared and it gave me comfort every time I touched it.' She fought to hold back her tears as she placed it in his hand.

'I don't understand, mother. Why are you giving it to me?'

'I don't need it any more. Do what you want with it. It took a lot of courage for me just to be here and say the things I've said. But I had to do it and I wanted you to share the experience with me.'

Antonio put his arms around her and hugged her gently. 'You're full of surprises. I never would have imagined we'd be having this conversation.' He looked at the coin, then dropped it in the pocket of his coat.

'Maybe now we can talk about the past — and I mean about your father — like two normal people,' she said. 'I'll still shed a few tears now and then because that's the way I am. The difference is that I'll no longer dwell on it like I used to and I promise you that I'll bounce right back.'

They talked for almost an hour. It was their first honest conversation since before Friedman had walked into his life. All the hurts, all the secrets of the past were laid to rest or at least put aside for another time. Afterwards, as he walked alone out of the park, he paused to look at the coin. Distorted images of his father flashed through his mind and he felt a sudden urge to throw it in the bushes. But he couldn't. It had meant too much to his mother and reluctantly, he put it back in his pocket.

On his way back to his office, Antonio passed familiar shops and businesses and stopped suddenly when his eye caught a glimpse of a coin on display behind a window of a rare coins shop. The coin looked remarkably like the one his mother had given him. Curious, he stepped into the shop to inquire about it.

'May I help you?' asked the owner, a man

in his late sixties, with a trace of a foreign accent.

'I'd like to see that coin,' Antonio said, pointing.

The owner obligingly removed the coin from behind the window and placed it on top of the counter.

'It's a very rare coin,' he said. 'Not too many of them in Mexico. If you're interested I can give you a good price on it.'

Antonio pulled out the coin from his pocket and put it next to the one on the counter. They were identical.

The owner's eyes lit up. 'Where did you get it?'

'I . . . I found it in a box in a friend's attic,' Antonio said. 'Can you tell me something about it? I don't know anything about coins and I was just curious to know where it came from.'

'It's an old Polish coin,' the owner said. 'It really has no significance except to the serious collector. I'll give you a fair price for it if you want to sell it.'

'Thanks, but I think I'll keep it,' Antonio said. 'If I change my mind, I'll know where to come.'

'In that case, would you be interested in leaving it here, on consignment?' the old man asked. 'That way, if a really serious collector should be interested in it, along with the coin that I already have, well, there's no telling what he would be willing to pay. You'd be surprised at the kind of offers I get for rare coins like these. There's no risk involved and you have nothing to lose. If you like the offer, you can accept it or not. The coin will always be yours to take back.'

Antonio thought about it for a moment, then said, 'Okay, I'll leave it.'

The old man smiled and quickly made out a receipt. 'You won't regret it and you may be a few pesos richer for it,' he said, placing Antonio's coin in a separate box.

As Antonio turned and walked out of the shop, he only casually took notice of a *mezuzah* to the right of the doorway.

*   *   *

It had been four days since Pamela had returned to Miami. If Ivana and Rosenberg were still out there, they were doing a good job of not getting noticed. But then again, Antonio wasn't doing anything out of character. From the time he left for his office, to the time he got home, usually late at night, he was like any other lawyer trying to juggle a busy schedule.

It was 7 p.m. and Antonio was still at the

office. When he heard the phone ring, he hesitated, then picked it up.

'Pamela,' he said, pleasantly surprised. 'I was just getting ready to leave. I was going to call you first thing in the morning.'

'I'm glad I caught you. So how are things going?'

'As a matter of fact, everything has been very quiet,' Antonio said. 'I've resumed my normal routine and, to be honest, I haven't noticed anything unusual. A few times I was tempted to look over my shoulder but I didn't want to appear overly suspicious. If they're still keeping tabs on me I want them to know they're wasting their time.'

'Good. That's really all you can do. But how long are we going to wait?'

'That's a good question. I really don't know. Let's just keep to our normal activities for a few more days. But stay flexible and be ready to travel the moment I call you.'

'Okay, if you think that's best.' There was a brief silence. 'I had another reason for calling. I . . . I wanted to apologize.'

'For what?'

'Well, about the video. I just wanted to let you know that it was really unfair of me to give it to you. At the time I wanted to be sure that you knew how really cruel your father had been, just in case you were having second thoughts about him. I shouldn't have done it. I shouldn't have doubted your commitment to doing the right thing. I'm sorry.'

'Forget it,' he said softly.

'Well, I know you were on your way out, so I'll let you go.'

'I'll call you in a couple of days,' he said. 'We'll see how things are going and then we'll just have to take a chance.'

He hung up the phone and gave himself a minute before getting up to leave. As much as he tried, he couldn't get the image of the old Polish woman out of his mind. He wished Pamela hadn't mentioned the video.

* * *

Antonio walked into his apartment, closed the door behind him and turned towards a darkened living room. That's odd, he thought. He was sure he had left a small lamp on. He took a few steps into the middle of the living room and suddenly a light came on. He saw two figures, one of whom he recognized as Ivana, sitting on the couch. The other was pointing a gun with a silencer at him.

'Sit down,' Rosenberg said calmly.

Antonio did as he was told.

'What's going on?' he asked.

'You know perfectly well why we're here,'

Rosenberg said. 'We're tired of playing games with you. We know why you sent Pamela back to Miami. Did you really think we would pack up and leave?'

'I don't know what you're talking about.'

'I said we're tired of playing games,' Rosenberg said. 'The two of you are planning on going back to Paraguay to look for your father. Aren't you? I don't know what she sees in you but you can't fool us. We know you're still in contact with your father and we want you to tell us about it.'

'You've got this all wrong,' Antonio said, shaking his head. 'I have absolutely no desire to go back to Paraguay. If you've been watching me, you know that I've been too busy working to think of anything else. As for being in contact with my father, that's ridiculous.'

Ivana was about to say something. Instead, she grabbed the gun from Rosenberg and pointed it directly at Antonio's head.

'Either you tell us what we want to know or I pull the trigger,' she said in a cold, steely voice. 'The choice is yours.'

'But I don't know anything,' Antonio said. He held up his hands.

In an instant she moved the muzzle slightly down and to the right and pulled the trigger. The flash from the muzzle, followed by the muted sound of the bullet as it hit just inches from Antonio's left shoulder caused him to flinch and utter a gasp.

'I told you I'd pull the trigger,' she said. 'The next time you won't be so lucky.'

'Okay, okay,' Antonio said. 'I'll tell you the truth. You're right. We were planning on going back to Paraguay to look for my father. We were just waiting until we were sure the two of you had left town. That's it. There's nothing else to tell.'

'You can do better than that,' Rosenberg said. 'We're not that stupid. Tell us about your father. Tell us how you've been keeping the truth about him from Pamela.'

'I don't know where you're getting your information but I can tell you it's all wrong. You were in Paraguay and you know as much about my father as I do.'

'You're in contact with him and we want you to tell us about it,' Ivana shouted.

'The two of you are crazy if you think I'm trying to protect my father. Do you think I'd betray Pamela and forget what my father did to her family? Do you think I can forget what he did to my mother? Think about it. I have as much contempt for him as you do.'

'That's very good, Antonio,' Ivana said with a smirk. 'Very convincing. But we're not buying it.' She thrust the gun toward him and aimed it directly at his groin. 'If you don't tell us the truth this very second, I swear I'll shoot your fucking balls off.'

'Look, you can kill me if you want, but it's not going to change anything. I've told you the truth.'

Rosenberg looked at Ivana, then reached into his shirt pocket and produced a familiar-looking coin. He dropped it on the coffee table in front of Antonio and waited for him to react.

'Where did you get that?' Antonio asked suspiciously.

'Is it yours?' Rosenberg asked.

'Yes . . . I mean no. It belonged to my mother.'

Rosenberg exploded. 'You're lying, you son of a bitch! That coin belonged to Schumann and he gave it to you. Didn't he?'

'I'm telling you, it belonged to my mother. You have to understand that — '

'I understand, all right,' Rosenberg said. 'Your father stole this coin and you want to know where he stole it from? Well, I'll tell you. He got it from one of his tortured victims whom he sent to his death. The man was a rare coins dealer who had sewn it and four others like it into the lining of his coat. I don't have to tell you, there aren't too many of them around, especially in Mexico. The

203

only way you could have got it was if your father had given it to you.'

'You're doing it again,' Antonio said, shaking his head. 'You're twisting things around to suit your own purpose. The fact is, my father gave the coin to my mother years ago, before I was born. She had it all this time and until this morning I never even knew it existed. She gave it to me because she wanted to break from the past and put his memory behind her. I know that's not what you want to hear, but that's the truth.'

'If what you're saying is true,' Ivana said. 'I'm sure your mother wouldn't mind talking to us and telling us all about it.'

'Leave her out of it,' Antonio said sharply. 'She's suffered enough because of what he did to her. What I told you is the truth and I would think you'd want to respect her privacy. She, too, was a victim of my father and it would serve no purpose to drag her into this.'

'Let me tell you something,' Rosenberg said. 'Ever since I found out about you, I always felt that sooner or later you would want to be like your father. That bullshit about being Mexican means nothing to me because I know that deep down inside you there's a German waiting to come out, and when it does, I know you'll come up with a thousand excuses for your father. And that's when I'll be there, waiting to tear your guts out.'

Rosenberg and Ivana looked at each other, then abruptly stood up to leave.

'Aren't you going to see us out?' Ivana asked, a mischievous tone to her voice.

Antonio got up and walked ahead of them toward the door.

'Give me a moment,' Ivana said to Rosenberg as he opened the door and stepped into the hallway.

Standing within inches of Antonio, Ivana smiled impishly and moistened her lips with her tongue. Her head cocked slightly and her mouth opened just enough, she moved forward to bring her lips to his. At the same time she dropped her left hand to the area of his groin and suddenly grabbed his testicles and squeezed them as hard as she could.

Antonio screamed as he dropped to the floor.

'That was just so you wouldn't forget me,' she said softly. 'Have a nice evening.'

She stepped out of the apartment and joined Rosenberg who was standing in front of the elevator.

'What was that about?' he asked.

'Nothing, I was just saying goodbye to Antonio,' she said with a grin on her face.

Dr Pacheco stirred his coffee, tasted it and then added another half a teaspoon of sugar. 'I don't mind telling you that this idea to start a new life certainly agrees with you,' he said to Elena from across her kitchen table. 'I just can't get over the way you look. You look like a new woman. I don't think I've seen you this happy in — '

'Go ahead and say it, in thirty years. And you're right, I haven't felt so alive, so much in touch with myself since I was that nineteen-year-old girl you used to know. And it feels wonderful.' She hesitated. 'This may be a little late in coming but I want you to know how much your friendship has meant to me over the years. You've put up with me and helped me during some very low periods in my life, even when you had more important things to worry about. In many ways, I took your friendship for granted. You could have walked out of my life at any time, and you would have been justified.'

'I wouldn't have done that. But I admit that more than once I had to ask myself if I was doing it for you or for myself.'

'And what was the answer?'

'The truth is, I kind of enjoyed being the one you turned to whenever you needed help, especially in the beginning after Antonio was born. I figured that as long as you needed my help you would always reach out to me and maybe, just maybe, you might begin to see me in a different way. So you see, I did have a selfish motive for wanting to keep up our friendship.'

'I'm glad you're being honest with me because it makes it easier to tell you that . . . I don't know how to say this without embarrassing myself. Maybe we can be more than just friends. I've been such a fool all these years and I never thought to consider your feelings. I hope you can forgive me.'

Caught off guard, he asked, 'Are you trying to say what I think you are?'

'Let's just say that if you were to ask me out for an evening, I would accept the invitation.'

He smiled broadly. 'I'm at a loss for words. You're going to have to give me some time to get used to the idea that you're available.'

'Well, get used to it because I've decided that I want to see and do all the things I've missed for most of my adult life. I want to go to Paris to see the Louvre or maybe ride a gondola in Venice. I want to learn a foreign language. I want to — '

'Whoa, you're making my head spin. I'm not as young as I used to be, and I don't know if I'll be able to keep up with you. Why don't we start with something simple, like dinner at a nice restaurant?'

'Wonderful,' she said smiling. 'Maybe I'll wear something elegant. I have a black dress that I've saved for just such an occasion.'

'You know, I'm seeing you and I'm hearing you, but I still can't believe the change in you,' Dr Pacheco said. 'You're like that sweet, wonderful girl I first met and — since we're being honest — fell in love with.'

She placed her hand over his. 'You're a warm, caring man, Ramón, and unfortunately I listened to the wrong voice in my heart. What a fool I was not to have recognized those qualities back then.'

'Have you talked with Antonio?'

She nodded. 'We met at Alameda Park and had a long talk.'

'Alameda Park? Isn't that — '

'Yes, that's where I used to meet Hans and it was precisely for that reason that I asked Antonio to meet me there. I had to do it. I had to confront those memories of Hans that had kept me from living a normal life. I had to break free of them.'

Dr Pacheco glanced at his watch. 'Listening to you and seeing this new side of you has made me lose track of time. I was supposed to be at the hospital ten minutes ago. I don't mind telling you that your coffee has never tasted better and that I may decide to make a pest of myself by dropping by every once in a while . . . for more than just the coffee.'

She smiled approvingly and squeezed his hand firmly.

'I'll see you at 8.30,' he said.

* * *

From his office, Antonio called Pamela in Miami. There was no answer. He tried again a half-hour later.

'I'm glad you called,' she said. 'This waiting game is beginning to get to me. How's it going?'

'Not very well,' Antonio said. 'Rosenberg and Ivana paid me a visit last night. They were waiting for me in my apartment when I got home from work.'

'What did they want?'

'They were predictable and came right to the point. They're pretty much on to us. The thing that really bothered me is that they still think that somehow I'm trying to protect my father. Everything comes down to my face, my *German* face. In their eyes, I'm guilty simply because I happen to look like my father.'

'Don't let it get to you, Antonio. What

they're trying to do is wear you down. For all we know they may have already left town. They knew they couldn't hang around forever, so they gave it their best shot. I say we wait a couple of days and just do it.'

'I don't know,' he said hesitantly. 'Too much has happened and I'm not sure that going back to Paraguay right now is the right thing to do.'

'You can't let a couple of Jewish fanatics intimidate you so easily,' she said. 'What they told you was all a bluff. If you back out now, it will be that much harder to try again when timing and other factors may not be as good.'

'You don't understand. It has nothing to do with Rosenberg and Ivana. I admit their visit shook me up, but it's nothing I can't handle. I know they were only trying to scare me.'

'Then what is it?'

Antonio leaned back in his chair. 'It's my mother. We had a long talk the other day. It's hard to explain, but she's like a different person. This whole business about my father, his reported death and then being told that he really wasn't dead has shocked her into making a very radical decision. She wants to put it all behind her and literally start a new life. I just don't want to risk doing something that might spoil her happiness.'

'You're really having second thoughts,

aren't you? I wish I could be more sympathetic, but after my father died, I made a promise to myself that I would finish what he started. I'm my father's daughter and I'm stubborn just like he was. Even if I have to do it alone, I'm going back to Paraguay.'

'Listen, don't do anything crazy. I just need a little time. I was thinking of taking a couple of days off to go to San Miguel de Allende. It's a small town in the mountains. When I get back, I'll give you a call and we'll take it from there. Fair enough?'

'Fair enough.'

'For what it's worth,' he said after a brief silence, 'I wish your stay here had been a little longer.'

'I was thinking the same thing,' she said softly. 'Just call me when you get back.'

20

Amsterdam

The old man seemed nervous and uncomfortable as he waited for the woman on the phone to finish her conversation.

'I'll be with you in a second,' she said to him, her hand cupped over the mouthpiece. 'Yes, Missus Leventhal, Mister Bergman knows that you have new information about Doctor Mengele, but he's a busy man and he may not be able to see you until sometime next week.' She nodded. 'You're right, Missus Leventhal, but I have a visitor and I must hang up.' More nodding. 'Yes, I'll make sure he gets the message. Goodbye, Missus Leventhal.'

She hung up the phone and looked up at the old man standing in front of her. 'She's one of our best supporters. She means well, but she's becoming senile. Keeps insisting that Doctor Mengele is still alive. She claims she saw him at the local market picking out a melon. Can you believe such — '

'I would like to speak with Mister

212

Bergman,' the old man said, very business-like.

'Is he expecting you?'

'No, but I need to talk to him about someone who may be of interest to him.'

'Can you tell me something about him? Is he a former Nazi?'

'I really would prefer to speak with Mister Bergman privately, if you don't mind. Just tell him that it concerns Hans Schumann.'

'Please wait here. I'll see if he can speak to you.' She got up and walked into the adjoining office where Bergman and his assistant were busy reviewing some files. 'There's a man here to see you, Mister Bergman. He looks very serious and he says it concerns — '

'I can't see anyone right now,' he said. 'Can't you see I'm busy? We're looking for a special document that has to be in Tel Aviv by tomorrow morning. Just take his name and tell him to come back tomorrow.'

'He says it's about Hans Schumann,' she said.

Bergman stopped what he was doing and looked up at her. 'Hans Schumann? He knows something about Hans Schumann? Why didn't you say so? Tell him to come in.'

The secretary rolled her eyes and walked back to her desk.

The old man was gone. She rushed back into Bergman's office and said, 'He's gone. I guess he must've changed his mind.'

'He couldn't have gone very far,' Bergman said. 'What did he look like? How was he dressed?'

'He was in his late seventies, wore a wrinkled, brown suit and . . . and he had a wooden cane,' she said quickly.

Bergman rushed out of the building and into the street. He spotted him walking away at a brisk pace and ran after him.

'Excuse me,' he said, coming up behind him. 'I'm Meyer Bergman. I believe you wanted to speak to me.'

The old man stopped and turned to him. 'I've changed my mind. It was a mistake. There's nothing I have to say to you.'

'Look, I know what you're thinking. You're afraid of getting involved in something that might cause a problem for you later on. Let's talk about it. I assure you that whatever you tell me will be kept in the strictest of confidence.'

The old man seemed uncertain and hesitated for a moment. 'Very well, but I don't want to talk in your office.'

'No problem,' Bergman said. 'There's a café up the street. We can talk over a cup of coffee.'

'I guess that will be all right,' the old man said.

They walked about a block and a half to a sidewalk café and took a table away from the street.

'We'll have two coffees,' Bergman said to a waiter who passed by their table.

The waiter nodded and scribbled a quick note on his pad.

'I want you to know that it isn't easy for me to be in this position,' the old man said. 'I wish he had asked someone else. But the fact is, he trusts me, and I feel an obligation to do this. To deliver his message.'

'I'm listening,' Bergman said.

'First of all, I think I should explain that I don't know where Schumann is exactly and besides, that is not why I'm here.' He looked around to make sure no one was listening. 'Perhaps I should start at the beginning. You see, when the Nazis were arresting every Jew in Germany, Schumann personally intervened and saved me from being sent to one of the camps. At the time I was a university professor and the whole thing, I thought, was a mistake. But it was no mistake. They had dug into my mother's past and discovered that she was Jewish. I won't bore you with all the details. What's important is that I owe him my life and I'm here to repay him in the only way I can.'

'You said you had a message to deliver,' Bergman said, impatiently. 'What is it?'

The old man hesitated. 'Schumann recently contacted me. How is not important. But he wants to surrender.'

'Surrender?' Bergman repeated, sceptically. 'I don't understand. Why would an ex-Nazi like Schumann want to turn himself in?'

'The truth is . . . he's dying. He recently found out he has inoperable cancer, and he doesn't have much time. Two, maybe three months at the most. He wants to come home to die in his own country. He made the decision shortly after his brother was killed by anti-Nazi fanatics who mistakenly thought it was him. He was very close to his brother and he blames himself for his death. He's all alone and he wants to come back home no matter what the consequences.'

The waiter appeared and placed the cups of coffee on the table.

'So what is the problem? Why doesn't he just do it?'

'Well, it isn't that easy. His fellow ex-Nazis would try to prevent him from doing it, for one thing. But the real truth is that he wants to surrender with certain conditions, and he wants to surrender to you and no one else.

He knows who you are and he trusts you.'

'What are his conditions?'

'He wants an entire day to be with his bedridden sister. After that, he will surrender to the German authorities and they can do with him as they like. Naturally, he would expect that you act as an intermediary throughout the whole process. Beyond that, there are no other conditions.'

'He must think that I can work miracles,' Bergman said. 'When the German authorities find out that Schumann is about to surrender, they are not going to be very cooperative. They will not stand for any conditions. I can tell you that right now.'

'Well, that is for you to work out,' the old man said. 'I'm just the messenger and I'm supposed to get back to him with an answer within three days. Think it over and let me know what you decide.'

'You haven't even given me your name. Where can I reach you?'

'I'll call you in a couple of days and if your answer is no, I'll just forget we ever had this conversation. If the answer is yes, I'll relay the message to Schumann and we'll talk again regarding the details. Now, if you'll excuse me, I'll leave you to finish your coffee. Please don't try to follow me.'

The old man got up from the table, looked

around and abruptly walked towards a waiting taxi.

Bergman gave himself a few moments, then got up, paid for the coffee and headed back to his office.

★　★　★

'Did you find him?' the secretary asked the moment Bergman stepped into the building.

'Yes,' he said curtly without bothering to look at her. He walked back to his office where Isaac was still going over the files.

'Forget about that,' he said. 'Something interesting has come up with the Schumann case and we've got some serious thinking to do.'

'By the look on your face, the old man must have given you some very good information.'

'He certainly did,' Bergman said. He pulled out a chair and sat down across from him.

'Well, what did he have to say?'

Bergman leaned forward. He repeated everything the old man had told him.

'But he's setting certain conditions, though. He's asking for an entire day to visit his bedridden sister. After that he will surrender, unconditionally.'

Issac's eyes narrowed. 'My gut level feeling

is that it sounds a little too good to be true. It could even be a hoax. And another thing, who is this old man exactly? What do we know about him? Can we really trust him?'

Bergman stroked his chin. 'You raise some very good questions, Isaac. The old man didn't give us very much to work on. We don't know anything about him except that he may be part Jewish and that he claims to want to repay Schumann for having saved his life during the war. I admit, it could be a trap of some kind, but we have no choice. If there is even a remote chance of bringing Schumann in, I'm all for doing whatever it takes, within reason, of course. When you think about it, we have very little to lose.'

'What about Pamela and Antonio?'

'What about them?'

'Well, don't you think we should tell them what Schumann has in mind just so they don't go out and do something that might jeopardize our plans?'

'Absolutely not. We can't take the risk. The two of them are too emotionally involved and they could become an unwelcome nuisance. For now, let's just keep quiet and let them do their own thing as if nothing had happened.'

'Well, then I guess that's it. When are you going to call the old man?'

'I'm not. He didn't give me his number or

even his name. He's supposed to call me in two days. After I tell him that I accept the proposal, he'll relay the message to Schumann and then we'll talk again.'

★ ★ ★

Alfred was in the garden tending his roses when the maid came out to tell him he had a phonecall.

'Who is it?' he asked, annoyed at the interruption.

'It's Señor Herman, from Paraguay,' she said.

'Tell him I'll be there in a minute.' He dusted the dirt from his trousers, scraped the clay from his shoes and then went inside.

'What is it, Herman?' he said from the kitchen extension. 'I'm in the middle of pruning my roses. They're like children, you know. If you tend to them while they're young, you get perfect specimens.'

'Yes, I'm sure,' Herman said. 'I'm calling because I thought you would want to know that Schumann is beginning to act like his old self. In fact, it's remarkable. Just a while ago, he was in the depths of depression and all he could talk about was wanting to go back to Germany to turn himself in. Now it's like nothing had happened. We don't know what

220

to make of it.' He paused for a second. 'But there is one thing, though. It could be nothing but then again — '

'What?'

'Well, yesterday, the maid overheard him talking to someone at the telegraph office, but she wasn't sure, exactly.'

'You may be right, Herman. It could be nothing. But we can't take any chances. Continue to keep a close watch on him. Do it in a way that he won't suspect anything.'

'I'll do what you say, but you should know that he's well respected around here and it just doesn't seem right to some people. To have to spy on a fellow German, especially a decorated hero like Schumann.'

'Just see that it's done, Herman. There will be time enough for apologies if we're wrong. And we may well be. For now, we'll just have to wait and see. If there's nothing more to discuss, I've got to get back to my roses. Call me if there's any change.'

21

Standing by the large, open doorway of the Church of San Francisco, Antonio looked at Father Quintana and shook his head.

'I still can't get over it, Father,' he said. 'I've been coming to San Miguel de Allende at least twice a year and I never knew you were here. All these years I thought you had gone back to Spain. It was a lucky thing that I decided to come inside to light a candle.'

'Antonio, luck had nothing to do with it. Your heart was burdened and you took refuge in the only place you felt truly safe and secure. And I'm glad you did because as sure as I'm an old priest from Segovia, your quest to find your father would have ended in tragedy for you, for your father and especially for your mother. Please consider my advice and don't do anything rash. Whatever you decide to do, I hope you'll stay in touch and maybe drop by now and then.'

Antonio half smiled. 'I will, Father. I don't know what it is, but just being here with you talking about my problems makes me feel like that little altar boy who used to squirm and giggle through every Mass. I miss those days.'

He waited a moment, then reached into his pocket and pulled out the coin his mother had given him.

'This is a rare coin that belonged to my father. I know it's worth some money. Exactly how much, I'm not sure. But I want you to have it . . . for the church. If anyone should question how you got it, just tell them that some troubled soul must have placed it in the collection basket.'

Father Quintana accepted the coin and briefly examined it. 'Are you sure you want to give it to the church?' he asked. 'Maybe I'll just hold on to it and if you change your mind you can come back for it and we'll say nothing more about it.'

'No, I want you to keep it and use the money that a good coin dealer will give you for it, to help the poor. Before I came here I really didn't know what I was going to do with it. For a brief second, I almost threw it in the bushes in Alameda Park. So you see, you're actually doing me a favor by taking it and I should be thanking you for accepting it.'

After exchanging goodbyes and well wishes, Antonio left the church and headed back to his hotel. By the time he got there, he knew what he had to do.

★ ★ ★

The next morning, Antonio arrived at his office around ten. He had overslept and was still feeling sluggish despite the two cups of coffee that hadn't quite done their job. His conversation with Father Quintana was still fresh in his mind and he wished he could put off making the call to Pamela. Would she understand? Probably not. But he had made up his mind and the sooner he told her and got it over with the sooner he could go back to living a normal life. He picked up the phone, punched out the first digits and suddenly froze. He couldn't do it. He had practically given her his word that he would help her and he couldn't just tell her he had changed his mind, not after everything they had gone through together. He returned the phone to its cradle.

Maria's voice suddenly came over the intercom. 'You have a visitor, Señor de la Vega. It's your mother. Shall I send her in?'

His mother visiting him unexpectedly? That's odd. Maybe something was wrong. 'Please show her in, Maria.'

Antonio stood up and walked up to greet her as she came into the room. 'Is everything all right?'

'Why shouldn't everything be all right?' she

224

asked. 'Can't a mother visit her son at his office if she happens to be in the neighborhood?'

'Of course. It's just that in all the years I've been here you've never paid me a visit.'

They sat on a couch next to a wall decorated with a group of framed photographs from the Mexican Revolution. She turned her head slightly and came almost eye to eye with the expressionless face of Emiliano Zapata standing proudly in full battlefield regalia. To the right of Zapata's picture was a photograph of Pancho Villa on horseback riding next to an open war wagon.

'I don't want you to think I'm being critical, Antonio. But don't you think such sombre photographs are inappropriate for the office of a successful attorney like yourself? If you want I can help you choose some nice paintings like a garden of beautiful flowers or maybe a view of the cliffs overlooking the ocean near Acapulco. Something to make your office look a little more dignified.'

'They were a gift from an old friend and they look just fine to me,' he said. 'But you didn't come here to give me advice on my wall decorations. What's on your mind?'

'Nothing, absolutely nothing,' she said with an upbeat expression. 'I really was in the neighborhood and thought I'd drop by to say hello. So don't ask me any more questions and don't worry about me so much. I'm fine, really I am.'

'Well, you certainly look it,' he said. 'I guess I'm still trying to make the adjustment after our conversation in the park. But I'm not complaining.'

'Oh, look at the time,' she said, glancing at her watch. 'I really have to go. Maybe I'll drop by a lingerie shop to buy something special for myself.' She smiled, then added: 'There's nothing like a silk nightgown to make a woman feel desirable.'

They got up from the couch and Antonio barely had a chance to say goodbye and kiss her on the cheek. She left as unexpectedly as she had arrived.

He shook his head and smiled and went back to his desk. He was still smiling when the phone rang.

'It's Doctor Pacheco,' Maria said.

'Put him through,' he said. 'Doctor Pacheco, what a pleasant surprise. Mother was just here and — '

'She was? Did she say anything?'

'What are you talking about? She dropped by to say hello. Is anything wrong?'

'No, nothing's wrong. In fact, things couldn't be better. But there is something that I need to talk to you about and I'd rather do it in person.'

'It sounds serious. I can go to your office or we can meet someplace in between, if it's that important.'

'It's nothing urgent, but it is important. Why don't we meet at Alameda Park. I'll wait for you by the fountain just across the street from the Belles Artes building.'

'Good. I'll see you there.'

* * *

When Antonio arrived at the park, Dr Pacheco was already there.

'*Buenos días*, Doctor Pacheco.' He reached out to shake his hand. 'You sounded very mysterious on the phone. What's this all about?'

'Let's walk through the park,' Dr Pacheco said. 'I'm sorry if I alarmed you. But it was something I couldn't discuss on the phone. It concerns your mother and me.'

'I hope the two of you didn't have a disagreement.'

'No, nothing like that. In fact, after we got home from the restaurant the other night, I would say that — '

'You took Mother out to dinner? Like on a date?' Antonio said, a little astonished.

'Why yes. Didn't she tell you?'

227

'No, she didn't. She came to my office but she didn't stay long. All she did was look around, criticize the pictures on the wall and then she rushed off to do some shopping. She was acting a little giddy — in a nice kind of way.'

'Well, if she didn't tell you anything, it will make it easier for me to say what I have to say.' He paused to arrange his thoughts. 'I don't exactly know how to begin. I think you know by now how much I've valued your mother's friendship over the years. And in her own way, I think she's valued mine. My purpose in telling you all this is because I intend to formally ask your mother to marry me. I don't know when, but I didn't want to do anything until I talked it over with you. This is a little awkward for me but I was hoping to have your blessing.'

Antonio stopped abruptly, and turned to Dr Pacheco. 'You're actually going to ask my mother to marry you? I don't know what to say.'

'I hope that means you approve,' Dr Pacheco said.

'Of course I do. Nothing could make me happier. The two of you are perfect for each other. For once my mother is getting the happiness she deserves.'

'I'm relieved to hear that, Antonio. Ever

since that night that's all I've thought about. I feel like celebrating, but I think I'll wait until I pop the question. By the way, I'd like to keep this between us. I wouldn't want her to know what I'm cooking up.'

'I understand. But don't wait too long or I might slip and say something stupid like, has Doctor Pacheco asked you to marry him yet?'

Dr Pacheco laughed, then became serious. 'There's something else we need to discuss. We talked about it before, but now that your mother and I will soon be starting a new life together, I think you should reconsider what it would do to her if you went ahead with your plans to find your father.'

'As a matter of fact, I've been giving the matter a lot of thought. I can promise you this. Whatever I do or don't do, my mother is not going to be hurt. Not if I can help it.'

They walked to the other side of the park, shook hands again and went their separate ways. Dr Pacheco's last comments left him feeling a little down, but he got over it by the time he got back to his office.

★   ★   ★

Bergman answered the phone and immediately recognized the old man's voice. He listened as the old man gave him instructions to be at a public phone three blocks away.

'Be there and wait for my call in exactly fifteen minutes,' he said, and hung up.

Bergman placed the receiver back on its hook and looked at Isaac standing across the room. 'That was him. He's being very cautious. He wants me to go to a public phone three blocks from here and wait for his call. Didn't give me much time. I'd better get going.'

He walked briskly and made it to the phone with a couple of minutes to spare. After a moment, he looked at his watch and put his hand on the receiver.

'Well, are you going to use it or not?' asked an impatient middle-aged woman who appeared out of nowhere. 'I need to make a phonecall, if you don't mind.'

'I'm expecting a call any second,' Bergman said. 'Can't you find another phone?'

'No, I can't. This is a public phone and I have as much right to use it as you do. Please step aside.'

'Look, if the phone doesn't ring in the next two minutes, I'll — '

The phone rang and he picked it up on the first ring. The woman glared at him for a moment and then stepped away.

'I'm sorry I made you leave your office,' the old man said. 'But I didn't want to take any chances. Just being in your office the other day made me nervous. Have you reached a decision?'

'Yes. Tell Schumann that I accept his conditions. When can I talk to him?'

'Not so fast, Mister Bergman. We'll have to take it one step at a time. I'll relay your answer to him and then it will be up to him to decide how and when. That's all I can tell you for now.'

'How will you let me know?'

'We'll do it the same way. Expect my call at the same time, at the same phone two days from now. I should have something to tell you by then. Remember, Mister Bergman, he trusts you and he's counting on you to keep your end of the bargain. Goodbye, Mister Bergman.'

Bergman hung up the phone, and hurried back to his office.

★ ★ ★

Antonio arrived home about 8 p.m., made himself a quick supper of shrimp salad and crackers, and put on a record of jazz tunes from the forties. All day long he had been thinking of Pamela and what he planned to tell her, and he needed the sounds of Basie, Dorsey and Ellington to distract him, for a while at least.

He ate while he listened to the music and didn't hear the phone ring. The shrill sounds of the brass drowned every noise in the room until the volume suddenly dropped and a bass player picked up the rhythm for an eight bar solo. The ringing of the phone cut through and Antonio heard it and rushed to turn down the volume and pick up the phone.

It was Pamela.

'I meant to call you earlier,' Antonio said apologetically. 'But I got busy at work and then I just decided to wait until I got home.'

'So how was San Miguel?'

'Great. Just what I needed. I ran into a priest that I knew when I was a little boy. Hadn't seen him in over ten years. We had a long talk and afterwards I did a lot of thinking. I realized that my reasons for wanting to find my father were no longer burning inside me like they were in the beginning. Too many things had happened since your father and I first met.'

'Sounds like you're calling it quits,' she said.

'I didn't say that. I just feel that for personal reasons, I should wait a while before doing anything. Who knows, maybe in a few months, I'll think differently. I'll just have to wait and see.'

'You've obviously made up your mind. I guess I have no choice but to go it alone.'

'That's crazy, Pamela. Maybe you should reassess your own feelings about this and try to do something else, something different for a while. What's the rush, anyway? My father isn't going anywhere. Six months from now or a year from now he'll probably still be in Paraguay.'

There was a long silence. 'There's a giant sculpture in Miami Beach,' she said in a slow, halting way. 'It's this huge hand reaching into the sky, and nude, emaciated-looking figures of men, women and children representing the millions who died during the Holocaust cling to the hand in desperation. It's an incredibly moving piece, that evokes feelings of anguish and pain. It may seem hard for you to believe, but I had never seen the sculpture until two days ago. Here I was, a Jew living in Miami, and I had never taken the time to see it. What I'm trying to say is that this whole experience has had an enormous impact on me and it has made me a better person, and more importantly a better Jew.' She paused. 'I really hoped you'd be there with me. But don't feel too bad. Maybe if I were in your place I would do the same thing.'

'I hate to leave it this way, Pamela. I want you to know that I'll always be here if you want to talk, or if I can do anything for you.' He finished with a few awkward words, then quietly hung up.

22

The lights in the basement of the old mansion flickered for a few seconds and then went out as Herman listened to the latest report on Schumann's movements.

'Damn this country,' Herman said. 'These people can't even run a simple power plant. Yesterday we were without power for almost two hours. What they need is a good German to run their power plant.'

'And their train system,' chimed in Otto, a German with a deep, raspy voice.

The lights suddenly came on again.

'Go on, what did he do next?' Herman said. He lit a cigarette and leaned back on the couch.

'Well, he went to this little grocery store that has a pay phone in the back and he made a call. He hung up after about thirty seconds and then made another phonecall. He must have talked for ten minutes, maybe longer.'

'Could anyone hear what he said?'

'No, but the young man I hired to keep an eye on him said he heard a few words that sounded German. After he finished his phonecall, he did a little shopping — milk, bread, that kind of thing — and then went back home. He didn't leave the house the rest of the day. The next day, he went to the same store and made another phonecall. He talked for about three or four minutes and then hung up and left the store.'

'Is that it?' Herman asked.

'No. I talked to his maid. You know that I bought her cooperation. She said that he spends most of his time reading and listening to music. Lately, he has been playing his Strauss records a lot, sometimes playing the same record over and over again.'

Herman took a long drag from his cigarette and exhaled slowly. 'From what you've told me, he isn't doing anything that unusual, except for the phonecalls. Is there a way to find out who he's calling?'

'For the right amount of money anything is possible,' Otto said. 'And for a few more dollars we can find out what's being said.' He shook his head. 'Do you think all of this is . . . really necessary? I feel uncomfortable having to do this to a fellow German. It just doesn't seem right.'

'Look, I feel the same as you do,' Herman said. 'I wish there were some other way. But the head council in Buenos Aires has decided we cannot afford to take any chances. For now, I think you should do whatever you have to do about the phonecalls. Now, if there's nothing else to discuss, I have to call Buenos Aires to give Alfred an update. I dread the thought that he might decide to bring in some extra help, if you know what I mean.'

Otto nodded and stood up to leave. 'I just thought of something else. Something the maid said about Schumann. She said he had been especially nice to her the past few days, nicer than usual. He asked about her family, how they were doing, things like that. He had never done that before and she found it strange. And he even gave her a generous raise for no reason at all. Anyway, I thought you should know.'

'Yes, I'm glad you told me,' Herman said, his mind trying to analyze the significance of Schumann's behavior. 'But what does it mean?'

Otto shrugged.

★ ★ ★

Maria's voice came over the intercom. 'Your mother's on the line, Señor de la Vega. Shall I put her through?'

'Yes, go ahead,' Antonio said. 'Hello, mother. How are you?'

'I have something to tell you,' she said. 'But first I want to ask you a question. What do

237

you think of Doctor Pacheco?'

'Well, he's an excellent doctor and people think very highly of him,' he said, trying not to let on that he knew what she meant.

'No, Antonio. I mean, as a person. I really want to know what you think of him.'

'If you want my honest opinion, I think he's a real gentleman. I don't know what else to say, except that I like him and I'm glad that he's been such a good friend to you over the years.'

'I'm so glad to hear that, Antonio, because — I hope you're sitting down — he's asked me to marry him. It all happened so suddenly that my head is still spinning. Just a few days ago, the idea would have been totally absurd. But now, well . . . it just felt good to hear someone actually ask me to marry him.'

'That's wonderful, mother. You said yes, I hope.'

'When he asked me, I was a little unprepared. I thought that if it happened, it would be after a few more evenings out together. But then he pointed out that we already knew each other better than most married couples and it didn't make any sense to wait. He's right, of course.'

'Well, so what did you tell him?'

There was a brief silence. 'I said yes.'

'For a moment, you had me worried.

Congratulations, mother. Have you set a date?'

'No, we'd like to wait. At least I'd like to wait a couple of weeks before choosing a date. I need a little time to get used to the idea that I will soon be Señora Pacheco.' She paused. 'Now that I've told you the good news, I want to invite you to come over for dinner tonight and help us celebrate.'

'I'd love to. I'll bring the champagne.'

* * *

Oblivious to the pedestrian traffic behind him and the noise of the cars passing by, Bergman moved up to the phone and waited. Seconds later, it rang and he picked it up.

'Hello?' he said, with a snap to his voice.

'I've got some good news,' the old man said. 'Listen carefully. Schumann plans to travel to Europe in four days. Once he arrives — I don't know what city — he will call you at the phone you are now using. Be there exactly four days from today at the same time as today's call. Is that understood?'

'Yes, I understand,' Bergman said.

'When he talks to you, he will give you additional instructions.'

'What kind of instructions?'

'I know, for example, that he will expect

you to meet him alone wherever it is agreed that he will surrender to you.'

'Anything else?'

'Yes, he expects you to keep his arrival in Germany a secret. No one from the German government must know that he even entered the country.'

'That will be difficult, but I will do my best.'

'Those are his conditions. If you can't comply with them, tell me now and we'll call the whole thing off.'

'Tell him that he's got my word. I will do exactly as he requests. Just let him know that as long as I am satisfied that he won't change his mind at the last moment, he will have my full trust and cooperation.'

'I think I can speak for him in that regard, Mister Bergman. He's made up his mind and there's nothing that will keep him from going ahead with this. I will stake my life on it. That's how sure I am.'

'Good. Then it's all set.'

'One more thing,' the old man said. 'He wants you to call his bedridden sister in Munich — her name is Eva Schumann — and personally reassure her that no one will interfere during his visit with her.'

There was a brief silence. 'I will call her. He can count on it.'

* ★ ★ ★

Isaac was standing next to an open filing cabinet when Bergman entered the room. 'Did he call?' he asked.

'Yes, he was right on time,' Bergman said. He quickly filled him in on the details.

'It's not going to work,' Isaac said, closing the drawer and shaking his head.

'What do you mean? Of course it's going to work.'

'How are you going to arrange for him to enter Germany without advising the German authorities? When they find out — '

'Who said anything about keeping it a secret from them?'

'You don't mean . . . but you gave him your word that you would honor his conditions.'

'My word?' Bergman said, his voice suddenly rising. 'Do you really think I had any intention of keeping my word to that man? He's a cold-blooded murderer and I would have said anything to make him believe he could trust me.'

'It still doesn't seem right.'

'Let me tell you something, Isaac. When I took on this mission I made a vow to myself that I would do my very best to locate as many Nazi war criminals as I could find. Beyond that, I held no reservations about how or what I had to do. And if it means making promises that I don't intend to keep, so be it. The way I see it, time is running out for those who are still left, and for me, as well. Look at me. My blood pressure is erratic and my diabetes is making me weaker with every passing year.' He gave out a sigh. 'I need to bring Schumann in. It may well be my last case.'

Isaac looked at Bergman and nodded sympathetically.

'I know what you're thinking,' Bergman said. 'But I want you to remember that we're dealing with someone who really has no right to expect any kind of decency from me or anyone else. He lost that right many years ago when he killed his first Jew.' He picked up the phone and dialled the number of the War Crimes prosecutor in Berlin. While he waited for the call to go through, he turned to Isaac and caught a disapproving glance from him. 'Well, I guess it won't hurt to ask if they would at least consider his request to see his sister.'

★ ★ ★

'Are you absolutely certain?' Alfred said, speaking into the mouthpiece.

'Absolutely,' Herman said. 'The person

who monitored the call said he heard it clearly. Schumann intends to fly to Europe on Tuesday.'

'That's only four days away. Good work, Herman. Don't let him out of your sight.' He hung up and quickly dialled Alexander's number.

After five rings, Alexander picked up the call.

'I just spoke to Herman,' Alfred said somberly. 'We have to meet. Call Josef and the two of you come over to my house immediately. I'll explain when you get here.'

★　★　★

Towards the end of the meal, Antonio raised his glass and gave a nod to his mother and Dr Pacheco.

'I would like to propose a final toast,' he said. 'May this day be the beginning of a lifetime of happiness and good memories for both of you and may you continue to celebrate the occasion again and again. *Salud.*'

'*Salud,*' echoed his mother and Dr Pacheco.

'Well, I'll say one thing,' Antonio said with a wide grin. 'The two of you didn't waste any time. Who would have dreamed we'd be sitting here celebrating this great occasion?'

'Your mother will have to take the credit,' Dr Pacheco said. 'If she hadn't nudged me into asking her to dinner, I probably would have been content to just stay friends like we've been for all these years.'

She blushed. 'Don't embarrass me in front of Antonio,' she said jokingly. 'But you're right. I did take the first step and I'm glad I did.'

'Have you decided where you might want to take a honeymoon?' Antonio asked.

Dr Pacheco and Antonio's mother looked at each other and smiled.

'We were thinking of going to Mazatlan for a few days,' Dr Pacheco said.

'Or maybe San Francisco,' she said with a twinkle in her eye.

'San Francisco would be great,' Antonio said. He reached over and poured the last of the champagne into his mother's glass.

'I don't think I've had this much champagne in . . . in more years than I care to remember,' she said. 'But tonight is special and the only thing that matters is that we're here together as a family just the way I imagined a real family should be.' She looked at Antonio. 'Thank you, Antonio.'

'For what?'

'For being so understanding and for

supporting my decision to do something that I should've done many years ago.' She paused to brush the tears from her eyes. 'I don't think I've ever been this happy. If I died tomorrow, I would die a happy woman.'

'Let's not get carried away,' Dr Pacheco said as he squeezed her hand gently. 'Nobody's dying tomorrow. Or the next day or the day after. This is supposed to be a celebration. Antonio, open the other bottle of champagne. The evening is still young and we still have a lot of celebrating to do.'

'Good idea,' Antonio said. He stood up, went to the kitchen and came back with a fresh bottle of champagne. He uncorked it and poured a little into his mother's glass and a little into Dr Pacheco's glass.

'Aren't you having any?' Dr Pacheco asked.

'No, the rest of the evening belongs to the two of you. Enjoy it and make it an occasion to remember.'

After a few hugs and kisses, Antonio left his mother's apartment and returned to his own. A perfect ending to a perfect evening, he mused, his mind temporarily shutting out all thoughts of his father and the unpleasantness of the past few days.

23

Amsterdam

Rosenberg walked to the end of the hall and stopped in front of the door with a DO NOT DISTURB sign hanging from the doorknob. He knocked softly and waited for someone to answer.

Seconds later the door opened and he stepped into the room. 'How's it going?' he said to Ivana as she closed the door behind him. He looked across the room and saw Eric, Ivana's associate, standing over an old man wearing a wrinkled brown suit. The man was slumped in an easy chair.

'He's dead,' she said without emotion. 'We only struck him a few times. He must have had a weak heart. It happened just moments before you got here.'

'Damn it!' Rosenberg said. 'I told you not to overdo it. We just wanted information from him. Now look what you've done. It's not going to be easy to drag him out of here.'

'Relax, Leonard,' she said. 'So he's dead. So what? He was just another Nazi collaborator and I'm not going to worry about it. We'll figure a way to get him out of here.'

'You were supposed to question him and find out what he and Bergman were up to and you failed,' Rosenberg said, jabbing a disapproving finger at her. 'Some day you're going to make one too many mistakes.'

'Who said we failed?' she said, a hostile edge to her voice.

'He told us everything,' Eric added. 'Just before he had his attack.'

'But I thought — '

'You thought wrong, as usual,' Ivana said sharply. 'If you're through trying to find fault with my methods, let me tell you what he told us.'

Rosenberg sheepishly backed down and sat on the edge of the bed. 'Go on, I'm listening.'

Ivana filled him in on what the old man had said. When she was finished, she added, 'Schumann will surrender only on the condition that he be allowed to visit his bedridden sister in Munich.'

'Bergman actually agreed to such a condition?' Rosenberg said. 'He must be getting soft in his old age. Did he say which city Schumann will fly to or which route he plans to take?'

'We asked him all that, but the old man didn't know anything more than he told us,'

Eric said. 'I really don't think he was holding back.'

'Well, at least we know the day he will call,' Rosenberg said, crossing his arms. 'It shouldn't be too hard to find out how they plan to carry out this secret surrender. We'll have to be careful, though. Bergman is a very cagey man and he's not going to run out and meet Schumann without taking all the necessary precautions.' He turned to look at the old man's body. 'We shouldn't hang around here any longer. Let's figure out how we're going to get him out of here.'

★ ★ ★

The Polish farmer, his wife and their daughter, a young woman in her early twenties, were eating dinner when the SS officer burst into the house and demanded to know why they weren't at the town square with the others. The farmer feebly explained that his family had not been told of the meeting and assured him they would leave for the square immediately. As the three of them stood up to leave, the SS officer stepped in front of the daughter and ordered her parents to go on without her.

The young, slightly-built, woman tensed up and avoided making eye contact with him, hoping he would decide to leave her alone. But the SS officer moved even closer to her, touching her face with his hand and ordering her to sit on the couch. Then he sat next to her and slowly began to fondle her, beginning with her breasts and working down to her thighs and finally to the area between her legs. At the same time, he kissed her on the lips, at first softly and then passionately, becoming more and more aroused.

Suddenly, he ripped her blouse open and reached for her breast. He grabbed it and squeezed so hard that it caused her to cry out in pain. He then moved his head toward the same breast as if to suck on it and quickly drew back in shock. Dangling around her neck was a small silver Star of David. 'You're a filthy Jew,' he said in total astonishment. He stood up and looked at her, his revulsion quickly turning into anger.

She sat there and made no effort to cover herself up. A small smile began to form on her face and she said half-tauntingly, 'What's the matter, don't you like my breasts?' She suddenly broke into a sardonic laughter and he shouted at her to stop. But she ignored him and she laughed even harder. She abruptly stopped laughing and became almost serious. After a brief pause, she said, 'Afraid to fuck a Jew, are you?' And then she broke into the same uncontrollable laughter.

'Stop it,' he said again and again. She didn't, and so he pulled the gun from his holster and shot her point blank between the eyes. He fired five more times until the whole front of her face was a bloody, obliterated mess.

Antonio broke free from the nightmare and sat up in bed, his hand clutching his thumping chest. It was the third nightmare in less than a week.

★ ★ ★

'Hello, Doctor Pacheco. I hope I'm not catching you at a bad time,' Antonio said, calling from his office.

'Hello, Antonio. You caught me in between patients, as a matter of fact.'

'The reason I'm calling is . . . I'm sure it's nothing, but I want to talk to you about a personal problem.'

'Oh?' Dr Pacheco said with a note of concern. 'What kind of problem?'

'Remember when I told you about a dream I had . . . about a Nazi officer who shot this man standing on the edge of a cliff?'

'Yes, I remember.'

'Well, I've had more nightmares. I had an especially bad one last night, and I wanted to talk to you about it in person if you can make some time for me.'

'Hmm, this is a little out of my field, Antonio. I'm not sure I can help you. But I have an idea. There's a psychiatrist who specializes in dreams and nightmares. He's a good friend of mine. I'll give him a call and ask him to set up an appointment for you this afternoon. How does that sound?'

'A psychiatrist? Isn't that kind of extreme?'

'Don't let the word frighten you. He's a very low-key person who will make you feel comfortable right from the start. Believe me, if I didn't think he could help you, I wouldn't be recommending him to you. Why not give it a try?'

'Well. I'm certainly not looking forward to another one of those nightmares. Okay, do what you can to set up an appointment for me.'

'I'll call him right now.'

★ ★ ★

'The Nazi was me, Doctor,' Antonio said, his voice suddenly dropping. 'And the girl was . . . Pamela.'

'Why don't we leave it there and we'll continue next week,' Dr Zambrano said. 'How do you feel?'

251

'I'm not sure. This is all new to me. To be honest, I feel like I've just gone through a very long confession with a sympathetic priest.'

Dr Zambrano gave a quick chuckle. 'You're not the first to make that comparison. Sometimes priests and psychiatrists do perform the same functions. But getting back to these nightmares of yours, I think we've made good progress today. Your recollection was above average, I would say, and that's a positive sign.'

'I was hoping you would tell me why I'm having them. They must have some meaning. Don't you think?'

'If I had an easy answer to give you, I would. Unfortunately, it's not that simple. That's why I'd like to take it slowly and try to get to the root cause of your dreams, rather than give you my impressions based on a single session.'

'But that's exactly what I'm asking, Doctor Zambrano. I know you don't want to give me any misleading information, but the truth is, I'm not sure I want to come back for another session. I just want to have an idea of what's causing me to have these nightmares. Surely, you can tell me something.'

Dr Zambrano looked at him carefully. 'I hate to go on a limb on this, but I'd say that a key factor may be a deep-seated identification you have with your father. You probably reject this intellectually, but somewhere in the recesses of your mind there is a need — the need of an abandoned child to be like his father. And you fulfil this need in your dreams which is a relatively safe and harmless place.'

'What about Pamela? Why did I see her that way?'

'You tell me. Is there something about her that you may be denying within yourself? Do you have any feelings for her? Does the fact she is Jewish affect you in some way?'

There was a long silence. 'I guess the answer to all your questions is that I'm not sure. I haven't really given it much thought.'

'Are you sure?' Dr Zambrano asked. 'Your subconscious recorded some thoughts about her, yet you seem unwilling or unable, to discuss it.'

Antonio shifted his body. 'A couple of times I thought about her in a way that . . . well, let me put it this way. I've had a few fantasies about her. But the circumstances were all wrong, and yes, her religion was also wrong, not that it really mattered. I mean, I wasn't looking for a romantic involvement with anyone. I just wanted to focus on what we had to do and I think she felt the same way.'

'I can see a connection,' Dr Zambrano said, nodding. 'These conflicting feelings you have about Pamela were played back in your dream in a way that is understandable.'

'Well, understandable or not, the question is, what can I do about it? Am I going to have to suffer through these nightmares for the rest of my life?'

'As I said before, I can't give you an easy answer because there isn't one. Your nightmares, as disturbing as they are to you, are only a symptom of what is going on within the inner layers of your mind. I hope you understand that if you don't deal with what has happened to you, you may experience a host of psychological problems for years to come.' He stood up to bring their session to a close. 'Think about it, Antonio, and when you've made up your mind, give me a call and we'll set up another appointment.'

Antonio stood up, shook his hand, and thanked him for being able to see him on such short notice. He left the office feeling that maybe he had overreacted when he called Dr Pacheco. He didn't need a shrink to tell him that his head was inside out and turned around as a result of all he had gone through the past few weeks. He didn't need to have his mind dissected and laid out to see what made it tick. No, he would go it alone and figure things out as best as he could. He shook his head. Who was he kidding? He needed all the help he could get, and he knew he'd probably wind up coming back to Dr Zambrano. But not for a while. Not for a long while.

24

Bergman kept his word and placed a call to Schumann's sister in Munich. He hated having to lie to a sick, old woman but he had no choice. The German authorities were preparing a trap for him, and in spite of requests to allow Schumann to spend a few hours with her, it was unlikely they would even allow him to enter her home.

A woman identifying herself as a nurse answered the phone. 'I'm sorry, but she's unable to take any calls. She lapsed into a coma late last night and she hasn't recovered. Are you a member of the family?'

'No, I'm . . . I'm just a friend,' Bergman said, stunned by the unexpected setback. 'How serious is it?'

'The doctor just left a few minutes ago and I'm afraid it doesn't look good. She's very weak and we're making her as comfortable as possible for the time she has remaining.'

'Well, can you tell me how long you think she — '

'It's difficult to say, but it could be at any moment. If you want to see her, you'd better do it soon. I'm sorry but I must go and see how she's doing.'

'Yes, of course,' he said. 'Thank you very much.'

He hung up the phone and looked at Isaac sitting across the room. 'Bad news, Isaac. Schumann's sister is dying. She's in a coma and she could go at any moment. If she dies before Schumann makes it to Europe, which is only three days away, he may not want to come in.'

'So what are we going to do?' Isaac asked.

'What can we do? We can't even call the old man to see what Schumann is thinking. If Schumann doesn't already know about his sister, he is certain to find out.' He picked up a photograph of Schumann and stared at it. 'We're so close to seeing this happen. We can't let it fall apart at the last moment.'

★ ★ ★

The phone was ringing when Antonio entered his apartment and rushed to answer it. It was his mother, anxious to break the news.

'We've set a date,' she said. 'I tried to call you at the office but you had already left.'

'That's wonderful, mother. When is it?'

'Next Saturday, exactly a week from today. Ramón left here just a few minutes ago. He took half a day off just so we could be together. We had a pleasant lunch at Delmonico's. What a beautiful place. I felt like a queen. Anyway, by the time we finished our lunch, we decided it was foolish to wait any longer and so we agreed on Saturday. Ramón even ordered a bottle of champagne to celebrate. I'll tell you, if I have any more champagne . . . '

'What about the arrangements? We'll have to hurry to notify all our friends. We won't have time to mail anything out.'

'It won't be necessary. We want it to be a simple ceremony at Ramón's house with just the three of us. At our age, why make a big fuss? I'll leave the big wedding to you whenever you decide to settle down and get married,' she laughed.

'Is there anything I can do? Why not let me plan the celebration afterwards?'

'We've taken care of that. All you have to do is be there. Oh, goodness, look at the time! I must go out and buy some eggs. I promised Ramón I would make him some breakfast if he dropped by tomorrow morning. I'll talk to you later.'

Antonio smiled as he hung up the phone. He turned to walk away when it rang again.

'Hello?' he answered, a smile still on his face.

'Hello, Antonio. It's Pamela.'

'Pamela. I didn't expect to hear from you for a while. How are you?'

'I'm fine. I was in the middle of practising my Spanish with the help of a 'Spanish-made-easy' cassette I bought at a flea market. Thought I'd give you a call to see how you were doing and . . . to let you know I'll be taking a flight to Paraguay tomorrow.'

'You're really serious about this, aren't you? I was hoping you would put the idea aside for at least a few more weeks. Is there anything I can say that will make you change your mind?'

'I'm afraid not. I've made arrangements for a guide to meet me when I arrive in Asunción. I also called Bergman. He suggested that I postpone my trip by a week. He even promised to send his personal assistant to meet me in Asunción if I held off. I told him I'd think about it, though I knew I wasn't going to change my mind.'

'You know, if he's serious about sending someone to help you, it would be foolish not to accept his offer. A few more days won't make a difference.'

She sighed. 'If I have to change my departure date by even a single day, I would probably go crazy. There's a possibility I would even back out altogether. Look, the real reason I'm calling is to let you know I'll be making connections in Mexico City. I'll have some time between flights and I thought we could meet . . . that is if you can make it.'

'That would be great. Give me your flight number and I'll meet you at the gate.'

'Air Mexico flight 907, arriving at 3 p.m.'

He jotted the information down on a piece of paper. 'I'll be waiting for you.'

★　★　★

Her attention focused on the small TV set that helped break the monotony of her job, the nurse waited until the commercials came on before getting up to check on Eva Schumann. She herself was in poor health, with varicose veins protruding from both legs, and she shuffled over to the bed to perform her duties. As she picked up the woman's wrist to check her pulse, she shook her head and muttered something under her breath. She kept her fingers on the wrist for a few more seconds just to make sure. Then she gently let go of the hand and turned to pick up the phone on the nightstand. She had to notify the attending physician that the old woman had died.

★　★　★

Rosenberg and Ivana entered the crowded restaurant and took the only available table towards the back of the room. They ordered a couple of sandwiches and some beers.

A half hour later, Rosenberg spotted a waiter pushing a cart filled with rich-looking pastries and he said, 'One of those apple strudels sure would go well with a cup of coffee.'

'Forget it,' Ivana said. 'We don't have time.'

'Just a small dessert, what's the harm?' Rosenberg said, trying to keep his voice down. 'Schumann isn't supposed to arrive in Europe for a day and half.'

'I told you before, we can't afford to fuck this one up. Not this time. Look, we're lucky to be here. If it hadn't been for Julia spotting Bergman and the old man together, we'd still be waiting and wondering what to do next. The girl deserves a medal for having the sense to follow the old man to where he was staying.'

'You're right, as usual,' he said grudgingly. 'I'll get the check and get my ass out of here. Don't want to be blamed for letting him slip through our fingers.' He looked around for their waiter.

'If you need me, I'll be at the hotel,' she said. She got up to leave and quickly sat back down. 'On second thoughts, maybe you should have some dessert.'

'What are you talking about?'

'I just saw Bergman walk into the restaurant. Hope he didn't see me. He knows me and if he recognized me, he'll know why I'm here.'

Rosenberg looked over her shoulder. 'Relax, he just took a table next to the kitchen. From where he's sitting, he can only see the back of your head. Looks like you're stuck here for a while.' He signalled the waiter. 'Sure you don't want to have some dessert?'

'Might as well,' she said. 'But make mine chocolate, anything with chocolate. It's my *other* weakness,' she said with a sly smile.

★ ★ ★

'Yes, I understand,' Isaac said, holding the receiver up to his ear. 'I'll give him the message the moment he gets back.' He hung up the phone just as Bergman walked into the room.

'Mister Bergman, I'm glad you're back. That was the War Crimes office in Berlin . . . a Mister Von Bremen. He wanted to let you know that Schumann's sister has died. But he said not to worry. They have the matter well in hand.'

'What the hell does that mean?' Bergman asked, walking up to Isaac's desk.

'Apparently they plan to keep the old lady's death a secret for at least a couple of days. They've arranged for her nurse to tell anyone who calls that her condition is unchanged, that she's still holding on.'

'Good,' Bergman said nodding. He turned and walked toward the window and looked out into the street. 'Now that we're getting close to the day, I'm beginning to get a little nervous.'

'Any particular reason?'

'It may be nothing, but when I entered the restaurant — you know the one I usually go to — I thought I saw a woman who looked familiar. I didn't think anything of it until later. I only got a quick glimpse of her. But she resembled a young woman who came here as a volunteer about seven . . . eight years ago. Let's hope it was somebody who just happened to look like her.'

'You say that like you know a lot about her.'

'She was a very idealistic young woman — a gentile no less. It didn't take long for her to discover that much of what we do is dull, painstaking research and not the glamorous field work in some Third World country she had imagined. I learned years afterwards that

263

she had tried to join the JFJ. I also heard through a friend in Israel, that for a price, she would work for almost anyone and do almost anything. So if it was her that I saw, we're going to have to be extra careful.'

'You said yourself that you only got a quick glimpse of her. It was probably not her at all.'

'Maybe,' Bergman said, still staring out the window. 'But let's not take any chances. From now on, every time you leave the office I want you to look around for anyone who may be watching us. But don't be obvious about it. I don't want anything to go wrong when I get Schumann's phonecall.'

25

From his living room, Schumann peered out into the early morning darkness and took note of a parked car with two men sitting in it. It was time. He went to his bedroom, packed a small flight bag with a few essentials and returned to the living room. He sat down at his desk and began to write a letter.

Dear Herman,

This is a very difficult letter for me to write because you and the others in this wretched country have always treated me like a brother. You have been my family through many hardships and I would never do anything to destroy the goodwill we have enjoyed for so many years. What I am about to do is the most difficult and frightening thing I have ever attempted. But I feel I must do it for reasons that are too complex to go into in this brief letter.

By the time you read this, I will be on my way to Europe. And soon after, I intend to surrender myself to the German authorities. Please try to understand,

Herman, that it was not a decision I took lightly. I agonized over it for days and finally convinced myself that it was something I had to do. With the cancer spreading rapidly, I just couldn't see myself withering away, day by day, knowing that I would never again see my dear sister or the country where we were once thought of as heroes. I am not afraid of dying, but I am afraid of dying in a place that is still as foreign to me as the day I arrived. I just want to be allowed to die in my own country. Rest assured that I will never betray any of you, so help me God. I will miss you all and I hope that after a few months when I am gone forever, you can find it in your heart to forgive me.

Your friend,
Hans

Schumann waited a moment, then folded the letter and placed it in a plain white envelope. On the front he wrote Herman's name and left it in the center of the desk. Then he picked up his bag and walked to the rear of the house and quietly slipped out into the yard.

★ ★ ★

When Schumann entered the terminal, he paused briefly to look for any familiar faces. He saw none and continued on to the International counter where he took his place behind a young boy and his mother.

After a few minutes, the woman behind the counter said, 'Next please,' and he stepped right up.

'I have reservations for the eight o'clock flight to Lisbon,' he said. 'The name is Schumann, Hans Schumann.'

The woman quickly checked her computer, and shook her head. 'I'm sorry, Mister Schumann, but your flight has been delayed due to mechanical problems. It won't depart for at least two, possibly three, hours.'

'I can't wait that long,' he said firmly. 'Surely there must be another flight.'

'Let me see what I can do for you.' She paused to do some more checking. 'Well, there is an Iberia Airlines flight with connections in Mexico City departing in forty-five minutes. But you'll have a very long layover before continuing on to Lisbon.'

'I'll take it,' he said after a brief hesitation.

★ ★ ★

'What do you mean he's gone?' Alfred growled into the receiver. 'You were supposed to stay with him and not let him out of your sight. If he shows up in Germany it will be a disaster. Do whatever you have to do, Herman, but find him.'

'I have everyone out looking for him,' Herman said. 'I'll call you the moment we have a lead.'

'Just find him, Herman. Find him before it's too late.' He hung up, waited a few seconds and then dialled a number in Panama.

★ ★ ★

The book was open at the page where a pressed rose marked a poem that she had almost forgotten. Sitting at the dining room table with the book in front of her, Elena wept softly as she read to herself:

The Silent Wind forever blows and
Brings to every heart a happy end.
  Gently
Breathing, oh so free. Softly saying,
Come with me.

The Silent Wind each day comes down
From high above the clouds that touch
  the
Sky. Seeking out each lonely soul.
Keeping love from growing old.

It comes to all who dare to dream of
Angels singing Cupid's song, whose
   melody
And verse just seem to want to say, it's
   your
Turn. Won't you come along?

Elena heard the doorbell ring and she quickly wiped the tears from her eyes. She took her time getting up to see who was there.

It was Antonio. He walked in and gave her a quick peck on the cheek.

'You've been crying,' he said. 'Is anything wrong?'

'Why is it that every time you see me cry, you automatically assume that something is wrong?' she said, mildly annoyed. 'I'm a woman, and women cry for many reasons that have nothing to do with being unhappy or something being wrong. If you want to know the truth, I was reading something that I had put away many years ago and I just happened to come across it when I was cleaning out a closet.'

He saw the book and walked up to the dining room table. 'Is this it?' he asked.

'Yes, it's a book of poems. Your father read a poem from it one afternoon and he gave it to me along with a rose.' She followed him and sat down and gently touched the rose.

'When I got home that night, I put the rose on the page with the poem Hans had read to me, and I closed it and put it away. Today is the first time I've looked at it since that night.'

He sat down across from her and glanced at the book. 'Maybe you should put it away, or better yet, why don't you let me take it and I'll keep it in a safe place.'

'I know what you're thinking, but I'm okay. Really. I can't go through the rest of my life pretending that I never knew him, that I never loved him. Things will come up now and then that will remind me of him, and I'll just have to deal with it. Ramón is right. Only yesterday he told me that it's better to talk about it than to keep it all bottled up inside. Believe me, I'm a thousand percent better off now than I was a few weeks ago.' She looked away for a second. 'You know, it's still difficult for me to understand how a man who can enjoy such a beautiful poem can be guilty of doing what people say he did.'

'Why don't we just let it go?' Antonio said, uncomfortably. 'There's no point dwelling on it.'

'You're right,' she said. She closed the book and put it aside. 'Let me make some coffee and I'll tell you about a few ideas I have for the wedding.'

'That's more like it,' he said with a quick smile. 'But I can't stay too long. I have to meet someone at the airport at three o'clock.'

* * *

Antonio spotted Pamela coming down a long corridor and he walked up to her and gave her an awkward kiss on the cheek. 'It's good to see you. How was your flight?'

'Good. Thanks for coming. I've got a couple of hours before my next flight. Maybe we can find a place where we can talk.'

'Two hours. That's not too long. Let's walk down to the main terminal. There's a bar where we can have a drink and you can tell me more about your plans.'

'I really have no plans,' she said. 'I know it sounds foolish, but I'm just going to play it by ear. When I get to Asunción, I'm sure I'll have a better idea of what I can do.'

'Well, whether or not you came here with the idea that you could make me change my mind, I have to admit I was kind of hoping to do the same thing with you.'

Just ahead, an elderly man in a gray suit paused to look at a city map on the wall. After a moment, he turned and walked away in the opposite direction. They'd missed running into Schumann by seconds.

★ ★ ★

They took a table at one end of the room, away from the noise of a large TV set showing a soccer game in progress.

'Two glasses of white wine,' Antonio said to the waitress who came up to their table.

'So *are* you going to try and make me change my mind?' she asked with a half-smile. 'You'll need longer than two hours, that's for sure.'

'Seriously, I did want to point out a few things that you may not have thought about,' he said.

'Such as?'

'Well, suppose, for example that you find out where my father is living. By the time you relay that information back to Bergman, you can be sure that he won't be there for long. The old German network will know everything you do, every step you take. They've already been burned once and this time they're not about to take any chances.'

She took a deep breath. 'There isn't anything you've said that I haven't already thought about.'

'Then why not reconsider what Bergman suggested? You could at least give it some thought and maybe spend a night or two here in Mexico. And when you're ready you can take the next flight to Paraguay.'

The waitress appeared and placed the glasses of wine in front of them.

'You talk a lot of sense. But I have a feeling that if — and I said if — I spent the night here, you would try to persuade me to cancel the trip altogether.'

Antonio picked up his glass. 'Maybe, maybe not.'

'I'm sorry but it means too much to me.'

'So the answer is no? What if I give you my word that I won't try to make you change your mind? I won't even bring up the subject. How does that sound?'

'Tempting. I really shouldn't . . . '

'I know this great restaurant where they have the best seafood in town. I'd love to take you there. You can pretend that you're on vacation.'

She chuckled and took a sip of her wine.

'Okay, but *only* on the condition that you won't try to make me change my mind. Tomorrow morning I'm taking the first flight to Paraguay and that's all there is to it.'

'It's a deal.'

★　★　★

After dropping Pamela off at a hotel, Antonio went back to his office to make a few

273

phonecalls and finish some work. He didn't have to pick her up until 8 p.m.

He was poring over a law book when his secretary stuck her head in his office. 'You wanted me to remind you,' she said. 'It's almost seven o'clock.'

'*Gracias*, Maria.'

Five minutes later, he put down his pen and got up to leave. If he hurried he had just enough time to go to his apartment, freshen up and head over to the hotel to pick up Pamela.

26

Antonio entered his apartment and suddenly froze. 'What . . . what are you doing here?' he said to the sombre-faced man sitting on the couch across the room. He took a few cautious steps towards him.

'Hello, Antonio,' Schumann said, standing up. His face was thin and pale, with soft frown lines around his piercing blue eyes and across his forehead. 'I know this must be a shock to you, but I had to see you. I'm on my way to Europe and I didn't want to miss the only opportunity I'll ever have to meet you. If you don't want me to stay, I'll understand.'

There was a long silence. 'I think you'd better leave,' Antonio said, a cold edge to his voice. 'It would be better for both of us if no one knew you were here.'

Schumann's face became taut. He hesitated, then started for the door.

'Wait,' Antonio said, unexpectedly. 'As you're here, we might as well sit down and talk. But I warn you there's nothing you can say that will make me change the way I feel about you.'

Schumann slowly sat back down.

'I want you to know it's not easy for me to be here,' Schumann said, 'but I had to see you, to see what you looked like. There's so much that I want to know about you. From the moment I found out that I had a grown son, I almost went crazy. The thought that I had fathered a son with the woman who had meant everything in the world to me, well . . . it just made me feel both happy and sad. Sad because I knew it would be almost impossible to meet you. When you arrived in Ascunción, I wanted to see you, but the others, the ones you met, didn't want me to come anywhere near you. It was their idea to substitute my brother, Rudolf, for me. If only I had argued more strongly against it, my brother would still be alive today and . . . I probably wouldn't be on my way to Germany.'

'You're going back to Germany?' Antonio asked suspiciously. 'I don't understand.'

Schumann took a deep breath. 'I don't have long to live, Antonio, and I want to go home to die and be laid to rest in my own country. There's nothing left for me in Paraguay anymore.'

'You're just going to fly into Germany like an ordinary tourist? Isn't that a little risky . . . I mean, considering you're an international fugitive?'

'I'm using an intermediary who has made all the necessary arrangements for me. You've probably heard of him. His name is Meyer Bergman.'

'Meyer Bergman?' Antonio said, disbelieving. 'He's your intermediary?'

'Who better than the man who knows all about me? Everything's been arranged. He's agreed to honor my one and only condition — that I be allowed to visit my bedridden sister. After that, they can do with me as they will.'

'I guess you have this thing all figured out. But I want you to know this doesn't change anything between us. As far as I'm concerned, you're still the man who abandoned my mother. What you did to her is unforgivable.'

Schumann sighed. 'You're right,' he said, softly. 'At the time I knew I was going to be in Mexico for only a few weeks, and I purposely avoided making very many friends. But when I met your mother, something happened to me, and I just couldn't stop seeing her even though I knew we could never have a future together. As God is my witness, I never meant to hurt her.'

'But you did,' Antonio snapped. 'And you never looked back.'

'You don't understand, Antonio. I was a

277

fugitive, and my only plan was to live as quietly as possible until arrangements could be made for me to continue on to South America. Don't you see? I couldn't tell her who I really was. Even if I had stayed, or even if she had agreed to run away with me, what kind of life would it have been for her? Having to move from place to place, never knowing who to trust, and always dreading the day when someone from the past would recognize me and turn me in to the authorities.'

'But you never even tried to find out how she was doing. You just left like a thief in the night. And like a thief, you stole her innocence and left her with nothing but bittersweet memories.'

Schumann buried his head in his hands as if he were about to break down and cry. But he didn't. 'I realize now it was wrong of me to leave her,' he said. 'But I only did what I thought was best under the circumstances. I figured the sooner I was out of her life, the sooner she would be able to get over it and meet someone else.' He paused. 'Did . . . she ever marry?'

'No. Thanks to you she became a semi-recluse. When I was a teenager, I kind of admired her for that. I mean, the fact that she never remarried. I always assumed that her love for who I thought was my father was so great, that she never considered anyone else. Only recently has she started to come out of her shell. She's . . . getting married in a few days.'

There was a brief pause. 'I'm happy for her. I really am. I only wish she had done it years ago. Who's the lucky man?'

'Doctor Pacheco. He's known her for many years and I know he's going to make her very happy.'

Schumann shifted his body and looked around the room. 'Do you mind if I ask a favour of you, Antonio?' he said, sounding a little unsure of himself. 'I know this is not exactly a social occasion for either one of us, but would you share a drink with me? Even enemies have been known to drink to each other . . . not that I think we're enemies.'

'I guess a drink wouldn't hurt,' Antonio said. He got up, went to the kitchen and came back with two tequila-filled glasses. He handed one to Schumann and sat down across from him.

They drank their tequilas in silence until Schumann spoke. 'I'd like to ask a favour of you.' He paused to anticipate Antonio's reaction. 'Would it be too much trouble for you to show me a picture of your mother? If you'd rather not . . . '

Antonio hesitated. 'There's a picture in the bedroom. I'll get it for you.' He went to his bedroom and came back holding a small photograph. He reluctantly handed it to him.

Schumann's eyes quickly filled with tears as he held the picture in his hand and looked at it. 'She's just as beautiful as the last time I saw her. Her eyes, her smile . . . she was like an angel to me when I most needed someone to lift my spirits.' He reached into his pocket, pulled out a handkerchief and wiped the tears away.

For a moment, Antonio almost felt sorry for him and wondered if maybe his father was telling the truth. Maybe he really did care for his mother.

'I never married,' Schumann said. 'You want to know why? Because consciously or unconsciously I always compared every woman I met to your mother. So you see, it wasn't just your mother who lost out. At least she had you, and maybe she was the lucky one. God knows, I've had my share of loneliness.'

Antonio reached for his glass of tequila and took a quick gulp. 'I want you to know that when I arrived in Paraguay,' he said haltingly, 'I was consumed with hate and anger towards you and I couldn't wait to face you. I had so many things that I wanted to say to you, not just about what you did to my mother but also about what you did to my friend, Harry Friedman and his family. But now there doesn't seem to be any point to it. Does it even bother you, I mean . . . the pain and suffering you caused to so many people?'

'I wish I had more time to explain the way things were for me and other Germans during the war,' Schumann said. 'It's easy for people to look back and think only in terms of black and white, right and wrong. But I'll tell you, it wasn't that easy, especially in the beginning. What started out as a noble idea quickly turned into something ugly. But we were trapped and by the time we knew what was happening, it was too late. It was follow orders or die.'

'You were only following orders, is that it?' Antonio said, his voice quickly rising. 'The Nazi criminals used the same excuse during the Nuremberg trials. You'll have to do better than that because that excuse didn't work for them, and it doesn't work for you now. The fact is, there is no excuse for cold-blooded murder.'

'I'm not trying to make excuses, Antonio. Of course I was wrong. If only you could put yourself in my place for a moment and feel what I feel. You'd know that it hasn't been easy for me, having to live with the guilt and the constant reminders of what I did to those innocent people, and I'm not just talking about the Jews.'

'If you were that bothered, why didn't you turn yourself in years ago?'

Schumann looked away. 'I don't know,' he said, shaking his head. 'Perhaps my desire to live as a free man was stronger than my conscience. If my brother hadn't been murdered, and if I hadn't been told that I had only a short time to live, maybe I wouldn't be here right now. I'm being honest with you because at this late stage, that is all I can be. I can't change who I am or what I've done. So, if you're going to hate me forever, well, that's the way it'll have to be. I'm not asking you to forgive me, Antonio. I am asking that you try to understand . . . at least a little.'

'I'm afraid you're asking too much, and if Friedman's daughter were here, she would probably say it's impossible. You may not realize it, but ever since people discovered that I was your son, I've had nothing but problems. People see my face and they see you, and they somehow assume that I share your views, that I think as you do. Too bad I didn't look like my mother.'

'Sometimes things happen for a reason. If you had looked more like your mother, none of this would be happening right now. Think about it. It was precisely because you looked like me that people made the connection between us. I'm just sorry that it all got out of control. Under different circumstances, we might even have been friends and I probably would have bored you with stories about your family, the German side, that is. I would have told you about my sister, my cousins and about my grandfather, Grandpa Josef. He was such a character. He loved to tell stories. All kinds of stories. I wish I had written them down.' His voice became softly wistful. 'I don't know why, but lately I've been thinking a lot about him and the rest of my family.'

Antonio gulped the last of his tequila and held the empty glass in his hand. 'Well, for you it will soon be over. I still have to live with your face, your German face. Somehow I don't think I'll ever be proud to say I'm part German.'

'Well, you should,' Schumann said emphatically. 'Germany is rich in history and culture. Not like most of these third-rate countries that I've had the misfortune of having to live in.' He placed his hand against his stomach and gritted his teeth until the pain had passed.

'Are you all right?'

'Yes, I'll be all right. I left in such a hurry that I forgot my pills. But I'll make it. A little pain isn't going to prevent me from going ahead with my plans. By tomorrow morning I should be in Lisbon and after that, well . . . I'll be in Bergman's hands.'

'How much time do you have? I mean . . .'

'A couple of months, maybe a little longer. You know how doctors are about these things. But it really doesn't matter. My life was over a long time ago. My only hope is that the Press won't drag you into this. If they do, you must explain to your mother that I never meant to hurt her, that I . . . well, you'll know what to say to her.' He glanced at his watch. 'I should be going,' he said, standing up. 'I don't want to miss my flight.'

Antonio sat stone-faced, afraid to show any emotion.

Schumann held up the picture he was holding and looked at it for a few seconds. 'It would mean a lot to me if I could keep it.'

Antonio nodded.

'Thank you,' Schumann said, dropping it into the pocket of his coat. 'I guess it would be asking too much for you to shake my hand before I go.'

'Yes, I think it would,' Antonio said icily.

'I understand,' Schumann said. He paused for a moment, then slowly turned and walked towards the door. A second before he reached for the knob, Antonio called out to him.

'Good luck . . . father,' he said, trying not to reveal his mixed emotions. 'You shouldn't have any trouble getting a cab at this time of night.'

'Goodbye, Antonio,' Schumann said, turning around to look at him. 'And thank you for calling me father.'

★　★　★

From the window of his fourth floor room, Antonio watched his father get into a cab and slowly disappear into the stream of moving traffic. For a moment the image of his father's sad, troubled face lingered in his mind, and he worried that maybe he had been a little too hard on him. But he didn't want to think about it. The last thing he needed was to feel guilty, or even sad. He turned around slowly and walked back to the living room. He needed a few quiet moments before heading out to pick up Pamela.

27

Bergman's secretary came rushing into his office, wildly waving a section of the newspaper. 'Did you see today's paper?' she asked frantically. She opened the section, and slapped it on Bergman's desk. 'It's him. The old man who came to see you. They found his body in a wooded area just outside of town.'

Bergman quickly studied the photograph and read the short article next to it. 'Police suspect he may have been murdered but they won't know for sure until an autopsy is performed,' he said, repeating the last line of the article.

'Who could have killed him, and why?' Isaac asked, standing across the way.

'Thank you, Amanda,' Bergman said to his secretary. He waited for her to return to her desk. 'The old man was probably tortured and forced to provide information about Schumann and his plan to surrender. That means that someone out there is watching us at this very moment. If it's who I think it is, we've got trouble, big trouble.'

'You're not talking about that woman you

thought you recognized at the restaurant, are you?'

Bergman frowned. 'I'm afraid I am. Her name is Gabriella but she calls herself Ivana. She's a professional and you can bet that she didn't come alone.'

'So what are we going to do?'

'I don't know,' he said, stroking his brow. 'We have to assume that they know everything. Tomorrow when I go down the street to wait for Schumann's call there's a good chance they'll be close by. All we can do is pretend that we don't suspect a thing. Let's keep to our regular routine as much as possible. Try not to look over your shoulder every time you go out of the office.'

'Maybe we should call the whole thing off,' Isaac said, a nervous edge to his voice. 'They've already killed once. Why take unnecessary chances?'

'For God's sake, Isaac. We're talking about a group of radical Jews who don't agree with our methods. Somehow, I can't believe they would try to harm me or you for that matter. We're all Jews and I'd like to think that it matters to them.' He looked away for a second, his face showing a troubled look.

★ ★ ★

287

The housekeeper opened the door and escorted Antonio to the study. 'I'll tell Doctor Pacheco you're here,' she said.

A few moments later Dr Pacheco appeared and reached out to shake Antonio's hand. 'By the look on your face, I would say this is not a social visit. Why don't we sit down and you can tell me what's on your mind.'

'He's here,' Antonio said, somberly. 'He was waiting for me in my apartment.'

'What are you talking about?'

'My father,' Antonio blurted out.

'But I thought . . . he's not here to cause trouble, is he?'

'He's dying and he's on his way to Europe. I guess he feels he has nothing to lose. I wasn't going to tell anyone about it, but I just couldn't keep it to myself. To be truthful, you're the only one who really understands how I feel right now and I just — '

'Where is he?' Dr Pacheco asked. 'How long is he going to be in town?'

'He's taking a flight to Lisbon this evening.'

'Good,' Dr Pacheco said, with a quick sigh.

'He caught me by surprise and I don't know if I did the right thing,' Antonio said. 'I mean, I didn't exactly make him feel welcome. I said some pretty strong things to him.' He shook his head. 'He wasn't like I had imagined him. All along I had this image of a monster who had no feelings for anyone but himself. He wasn't like that at all. In a way it would have been easier for me to deal with it if he had been . . . a monster, that is.'

'You don't have to explain, Antonio. I understand. Maybe it's good that he came to see you. At least you no longer have to wonder about him and whether you should go out to look for him.'

'I just can't get over seeing him break down the way he did. He took one look at mother's picture and he — '

'You showed him a picture of your mother?'

'He asked, and I showed him a small one taken a couple of months ago. When he asked if he could keep it, I didn't know what to say, so I let him have it.'

Dr Pacheco paused. 'Are you absolutely sure he's leaving tonight?'

'That's what he told me. He's got it all planned out. He has to be in Lisbon by tomorrow morning. I know what you're thinking but I don't think he wants to hang around here too long. He knows that his friends from Paraguay will soon be looking for him to try to take him back. He left a little while ago, so he should be halfway to the airport.'

The housekeeper walked into the study

and interrupted them. 'Excuse me, Doctor Pacheco, Señora de la Vega is on the phone.'

'Thank you, Marta, I'll take it on the extension.' He turned to Antonio. 'We call each other every night about this time.'

'Go ahead and talk to her. I'm late as it is and I've got to be going. I'll see myself to the door. Maybe I'll call you later.' He turned around and slowly walked out of the room.

Dr Pacheco waited a couple of seconds, then picked up the phone. 'Hello, Elena. I was just saying goodbye to Antonio when you called. He . . . he was here to borrow one of my medical books, for some case he's working on, I suppose.'

'I think he works too hard,' she said. 'I wish he would spend some of that energy on finding a wife for himself. Maybe you should talk to him some day, or better yet, introduce him to one of your pretty nurses.'

'Believe me, Elena, Antonio does not need my help in finding women. He's a grown man and when he's ready, he'll find the right person and settle down. I have no doubt that you will be a grandmother some day, a very attractive grandmother if I may say.' He paused for a second. 'Listen, I know it's a little late but what do you say if I drop by and we can go out for a cappuccino?'

'At this hour? Why don't we put it off until

tomorrow? I need to see you anyway, to show you some patterns that I've selected for some new silverware.'

'Good, you can show them to me tonight. I can be there in fifteen minutes.'

'I'd really rather not, Ramón. I'm kind of tired and I just want to relax a little before going to bed. Is anything the matter? You sound a little anxious.'

'No, nothing's the matter,' he said, unconvincingly. 'You're right. It's too late to go out. I'll call you in the morning or maybe I'll drop by for coffee.'

'I'll have it waiting for you along with a couple of those corn muffins that you like so much.'

After he had hung up the phone, Dr Pacheco waited a moment, then called out to his housekeeper. 'Marta,' he said, a worried look on his face. 'Make me a strong cup of coffee. I think I'll stay up for a while.'

★ ★ ★

Sitting in the back of the cab as it sped toward the airport Schumann reached into his pocket and pulled out the photograph of Elena. After a moment, he put it away and leaned forward to get the driver's attention.

291

'I want you to turn around,' he said. 'Take me to the Polanco area. And if you know of a good gift shop along the way, pull over and stop. I need to buy a small gift.'

'Whatever you say, señor,' the driver said, nodding to the image in his rearview mirror.

★   ★   ★

'Wait for me,' Schumann said, getting out of the car. The sign over the doorway of the shop said: 'A Place For The Home, Antiques and Fine Gifts'. Schumann walked in and began to browse through the small store run by two elderly ladies with a penchant for cats. There were cats in ceramic, bronze, clay, exotic woods and many other materials. They were displayed almost everywhere. In the corner, atop a pile of thick, multicolored cushions, was the real thing, a lazy-looking calico with its eyes partially open, oblivious to everything around him, including the over-filled dish of food in front of him.

'Is there something I can help you with?' one of the ladies asked. 'We have things from all over the world, as you can see.'

'I'm looking for a music box,' Schumann said. 'One that plays a waltz.'

'We have a fine English box that just came in last week. It plays a beautiful melody.

I Love You Truly, I think. I can show it to you if you'd like.'

'No, no,' he said impatiently. 'It has to play a waltz.'

The old lady paused for moment. 'Wait here. You may be in luck. It's one of our finer pieces that we keep for serious collectors.' She disappeared into the back room and returned a few moments later, holding a sterling silver antique box in the shape of a baby grand piano. She turned the key a few times, opened the lid, and waited for the mechanism to produce the first notes.

A smile crossed Schumann's face as he heard the familiar opening to the *Blue Danube Waltz*. 'I'll take it,' he said, reaching for his wallet.

★　★　★

Antonio entered the lobby and spotted Pamela sitting on the edge of a couch. 'I'm sorry I'm late,' he said as he walked up to her and sat down beside her.

'That's all right. I figured you got tied up with one of your clients.'

He ran his fingers through his hair and loosened his tie. 'Listen. There's something you should know,' he said, slowly. 'After I left my office I went back to my apartment and when I opened the door . . . I saw him sitting on the couch, waiting for me. It just freaked me out.'

'Saw whom?' she asked.

He paused and said softly, 'My father. My first reaction was to kick him out of the apartment, but something inside told me that I had to give him a chance to explain himself.'

'You actually met him, face to face?' she said, her jaw dropping slightly. 'I don't understand. What is he doing here? You didn't just let him get away, did you?'

'He's not getting away, as you put it. He's very ill and he's only got a short time to live. He's taking a plane to Europe tonight. No one knows anything about it except . . . except Bergman.'

'What does Bergman have to do with this?'

'Apparently he made some kind of deal with him to turn himself in. I know it sounds crazy but he wanted Bergman to be his intermediary. He's the only one he could trust to handle his surrender and his request to see his bedridden sister.'

'I . . . don't know what to say. If you hadn't talked me into staying over, I would have gone to Paraguay for nothing. So what did he want?'

'I told you. He wanted to meet me. I don't

know what he expected, but what he got was a very cold reception. By the time he left, he knew I had no feelings for him whatsoever, at least not the kind he had hoped for.' He looked away for a moment. 'Let me tell you. It was tough. For a while, I didn't know how much I could take, listening to him talk about my mother and about his excuse for having been a part of something so evil.'

'How long does he have?' she asked.

'Two, three months at the most.'

'Maybe I'm more cynical than you are, but how do you know he was telling the truth . . . about anything?'

Antonio let out a sigh. 'There was something about his eyes. I don't know how to explain it but the way he looked at me, well . . . I just knew he was being honest. He didn't act or look like the brutal Nazi who murdered your father's family, that's for sure. Maybe it was because of his age or because of his illness. A beaten man is what comes to mind.'

'You're not feeling sorry for him, are you?'

'Maybe. Does that surprise you? It does me.'

There was a brief pause. 'Maybe he is telling the truth,' she said. 'But I wish there was a way to make sure that he isn't trying to — '

'To what? Why would he knowingly take such a risk? He's left the only safe place he's ever known since the war. He wouldn't have done that if he didn't have a good reason. He knows perfectly well what's ahead of him.'

Pamela stood up. 'There is one way to find out if he's telling the truth.'

'I thought of that.'

'There's a phone over there,' she said, nodding across the room. 'Let's call him right now.'

They walked over to a courtesy phone next to the front desk. Pamela picked up the receiver, gave the operator instructions and waited for the call to go through.

'Mister Bergman. It's Pamela Friedman,' she said. 'I'm here in Mexico City with Antonio and we thought you should know . . . Hans Schumann is in town.'

'How do you know that?' Bergman asked cautiously. 'Have you seen him?'

'He showed up at Antonio's apartment and he claimed he was on his way to Europe to meet you.'

'Damn it!' Bergman said. 'I was afraid of something like this.'

'Then he *is* telling the truth. Why did you keep it from me the other night when I called you?'

'Never mind about that,' Bergman said.

'Where is he now?'

'He should be at the airport.'

'Look, I don't have time to explain, but it's important that Schumann gets on that plane tonight. Go to the airport immediately and see if you can spot him. But don't go near him. Call me the moment you see him board the plane. Is that clear?'

Pamela nodded. 'I understand,' she said and hung up.

'We don't have time to lose,' she said, turning to Antonio. 'Let's get a cab.'

28

Elena was in the bedroom when she heard the doorbell ring. It was late, too late for anyone she knew to be ringing her door. She hesitated, then walked into the living room.

When she opened the door, she let out a quick gasp and took a step backwards. 'Hans,' she said, her eyes quickly welling up with tears. 'Is it really you?'

'It's been a long time, Elena. You look as beautiful as the last time I saw you.'

★　★　★

Antonio and Pamela walked up to the International counter and checked the schedule of outgoing flights.

'There's a flight leaving for Lisbon at 10.30 p.m.,' Antonio said. 'That has to be it.' He turned to the young woman behind the counter, put on his best smile and said, 'Excuse me, I know this may sound a little strange, but my father is supposed to take the ten-thirty flight to Lisbon and . . . well, we had a disagreement earlier in the day and I wasn't sure if he had changed his mind. I

298

wonder if you could check to see if he's still scheduled to take that flight. I was hoping to see him and patch things up. His name is Hans Schumann.'

'I'm sorry, it's against regulations,' she said with a sympathetic smile. She looked to her left, then to her right. 'Just a second.' Her nimble fingers quickly typed a command on her keyboard. 'He's still on the passenger list,' she said viewing her blinking monitor. 'By the way, there was a man who came by earlier inquiring about him. I didn't like his looks, so I told him I couldn't help him.'

'What did he look like?'

'Well, he looked European, in his mid-forties and he had an accent, German, I would say. As I recall he was wearing khaki pants.'

'Thanks,' Antonio said. He followed Pamela to a waiting area across the way. They sat opposite a teenage boy and his parents, American tourists, waiting to take a late-night flight back to the US.

'This obviously isn't going to be as easy as I thought,' Antonio said. He scanned the people around him.

'So what are we going to do?' Pamela said. 'When Schumann shows up, this guy is probably going to try to kidnap him right there on the spot.'

'Why don't we start by splitting up? You stay here and I'll go to the other side,' he said, pointing across the terminal. 'As soon as we spot my father we'll walk right up to him and stay close until he's safely behind the security check-point. The man wouldn't dare try anything in front of two highly visible witnesses.'

★ ★ ★

'I didn't plan to see you . . . not that I didn't want to,' Schumann said, sitting on the couch next to Elena. 'I was afraid that I would stir up unpleasant memories. But I didn't want to leave Mexico without seeing you, if only for a few moments. I already saw Antonio. It was a difficult thing to do . . . to meet the son that I never knew I had. We didn't know what to say to each other, but we did share a drink together. You did a good job, Elena. I'm only sorry that I wasn't there to help you. If only I had known — '

'Oh, Hans, what difference would it have made? You were running away from something I didn't understand until a few days ago. All I know was that my life came to an end the day you left. I fell in love with you almost from the first day we met, and I would have followed you to the end of the world.

Surely, you must have known that. I guess what still bothers me to this day is why . . . why did you leave? Was it because you were running, or because you never really meant all those things you said to me?'

Schumann moved his hand toward hers and stopped abruptly. 'What I felt for you back then was real, Elena. You have to believe me. At the time, I didn't know what was going to happen to me and for a while I didn't care because I had you and that's all that mattered. Unfortunately, I took the easy way out and I've been sorry ever since. But I never stopped loving you. I want you to know that.'

'And I never stopped loving you, Hans. Not even when I finally realized that you weren't coming back. It was hard, very hard to let go of the memories, especially of our last night together. As I grew older, I tried to suppress those memories. Of course, I never really could. But now I've learned to put the past where it belongs and I no longer have to fear new things, new adventures. I'm even thinking of taking piano lessons.'

'Good for you. Life is too short to put off doing the things that really count. No one knows that better than I.'

'I'm glad to hear you say that, Hans, because . . . I don't know how to say this but there's someone in my life that I've become very fond of and — '

'I heard,' he said. 'He's a lucky man. You deserve all the happiness in the world.'

'I'm the one who's lucky because I feel that I'm getting a second chance. I may not feel as romantic as I did when I was a young girl but somehow it doesn't matter. I think what's important is that Ramón and I care for each other in a way that is perhaps more meaningful, more realistic.'

'It almost sounds like you're not really in love with him,' he said. 'I'm sorry, I shouldn't have said that. It's none of my business and I have no right to know the answer.'

'On the contrary. You should know and I want you to know. Ramón is well aware that I'll never have the same feelings for him that I had for you. Nothing can take that away from me, Hans, and no one can take the place you occupied in my heart for so many years.'

'I'm sorry I brought it up. Please forgive me.'

She smiled softly. 'It's all right. I'm comfortable with it. That's why I'm being so honest with you.' She paused. 'You haven't said what you're doing in Mexico. Aren't you afraid someone might recognize you and — '

The phone rang and she hesitated for a moment before getting up to answer it.

302

It was Dr Pacheco.

'Everything is fine,' she said, standing next to a small writing desk. 'Of course I'm alone. I was . . . just about to get ready to go to bed. If there was anything wrong I would have called you. It's late, Ramón. I'm sure you're as tired as I am so let's just say goodnight and we'll see each other tomorrow morning.'

She hung up the phone and walked back to the couch. 'I hate having to lie to him. He's such a dear man. Tomorrow I'll tell him all about it.'

'And what will you tell him?'

'The truth. That you dropped by unexpectedly and that we talked about something that happened many years ago.'

He moved closer to her and reached out to touch her face with his hand. 'Maybe it was a mistake for me to come here. Seeing you again after all these years. It's like time never passed. I feel exactly the same as the day we met.' He reached over to kiss her on the lips and she turned away from him.

'I'm sorry,' he said. 'I don't know why I did that. I don't want you to think that I came here for any other reason than to see you one last time.'

She smiled. 'You still haven't told me what you're doing in Mexico?'

'I . . . had some business to take care of,' he

303

said, trying to come up with something halfway believable. 'A friend of mine who's very ill wanted me to do him a favor. He wanted me to deliver some important papers, a Will, bank statements, things like that, to his only living relative. He lives not too far from here. I only planned to be in town a few hours and I was afraid to even consider seeing you and Antonio. But I'm glad I did.'

'I'm not sure I feel the same way, Hans. You were out of my life for all these years and I honestly never thought I'd ever see you or hear from you again. I'm a lot stronger now, otherwise I don't think I would be able to handle it. You could have come back any time, but you chose to see me only because you happened to be in town. Can't you see how that would make me feel?'

'I don't have a good answer, Elena, because . . . I wish I could explain. The truth is, I wanted to see you and I never even considered that you wouldn't want to see me. It was very presumptuous of me, I know, and I'm sorry if I did the wrong thing by coming here.'

She looked away for a moment, then said, 'I suppose Antonio told you that I never said anything to him about your being his father.'

'I'm sure he doesn't hold it against you. In

fact, he's very protective of you and I admire him for that. I'm only sorry that he and I didn't get to know each other a little better. When I first saw his face I naïvely assumed that it would somehow make it easier for us to identify with one another. But I guess it was too much to hope for. To him, I'm his biological father, nothing more. Not that I was expecting a warm welcome from him.'

'You have to understand that he learned about your past at the same time he learned you were his father. It's a kind of thing you don't get over easily. I'm just thankful that having everything out in the open hasn't changed anything between us. In fact, I think it's brought us a little closer.'

'I'm glad to hear that,' he said, glancing at his watch. 'Maybe in the future, you can tell him that no matter what he thinks of me, I'll always be proud to be his father.'

★ ★ ★

Their car was parked a block and a half away from the Nazi Documentation Center building. It was partially hidden by a large tree with wide bushy branches that extended to the top of the windshield. Perfect cover to sit and wait. Rosenberg was the first to notice that someone in Bergman's office had the

305

habit of looking out the window for no apparent reason.

'It's like he's looking for a surveillance,' he said to Ivana sitting next to him. 'You don't suppose they know, do you?'

'So what if they do?' she said matter-of-factly. 'If I know Bergman, he's not going to let a little surveillance get in the way of bringing in a fugitive like Schumann. He's probably sitting at his desk at this very moment trying to figure out a way to outsmart us. As far I'm concerned it will make the game just that much more interesting. Relax and keep your eyes on that building.'

'A game?' Rosenberg said, annoyed at her cavalier attitude. 'Is that all it is to you? I know that you're good at what you do, but I don't think you take our work as seriously as you should.'

'Look, I don't need you or anyone else to lecture me about our work. You don't have the balls to do what I do and until you get a pair, I don't want to hear any shit from you about my choice of words. Is that clear enough for you?'

Rosenberg flushed. He held back from saying something he knew he'd probably regret.

★ ★ ★

'Get away from that window!' Bergman yelled. 'The way you keep getting up to look out every ten minutes is beginning to get on my nerves. They're not going to be standing in the middle of the street with a pair of binoculars. Just sit down and find something to do. This waiting is getting to me, too. Until we know that Schumann is on that plane, we can't worry about what Ivana and her friends might try to do.'

'What if he doesn't make it?' Isaac said, walking back to his desk. 'What if he has a change of heart and decides to go back to Paraguay?'

'He's going to make it, Isaac. I just know it. If for no other reason than to see his sister one last time.' He looked at his watch. 'It won't be long now.'

★ ★ ★

Antonio walked back over to where Pamela was sitting and sat next to her. 'It's a little over an hour before departure. He still has time, but he'd better hurry.'

'Any sign of that man?' she asked.

'Nothing. If he's here, he's doing a good job of staying out of sight.'

'I hope we're not being misled somehow,' she said.

'What do you mean?'

'Well, how do we know your father is really going to go through with this? It could be . . . I don't know . . . some kind of ploy. Maybe one of us should get on the plane, just in case.'

He turned to her and said, 'Listen, as far as I'm concerned, it's over the moment he steps onto that plane. I think it took a lot of courage for him to get this far, and I seriously doubt that he's going to change his mind or pull some kind of last-minute stunt. I'm the one who talked to him and I'm telling you he's dead set on going back to Germany.'

'You're probably right. It's this waiting that's causing me to question every little thing. I'll feel better when he shows up and we see him pass through the security checkpoint.'

Minutes later, Antonio looked at her and said, 'On the way to the airport I thought about the first time I saw you. For some reason it seems that I've known you for a much longer time than I really have. It's too bad we never really had a chance to talk about other things . . . like the kind of movies you like, the type of music you enjoy. I don't even know if you like Mexican food.'

She chuckled. 'I think I know what you're trying to say and I feel the same way.'

'You do?' he said. He suddenly caught a glimpse of a man coming out of a gift shop. He was wearing khaki pants and fitted the general description of the man who had been inquiring about his father. He kept looking around, like he was anxious about something, and then he went into another gift shop.

'Come on,' Antonio said. 'Let's check out that guy.' They walked across the lobby and stopped a few feet from the shop's entrance.

'What do you think?' he asked, his eyes focused on the man inside.

'If it's him I hope he didn't see us sitting back there,' she said. 'He could have recognized you and figured we were all here for the same reason. Wait, he looks like he's about to come out. Let's walk in here before he sees us.' They scooted into a gold and silver store and watched him come out of the gift shop. Seconds later, they saw him stop abruptly and come face to face with a tall, robust-looking priest accompanied by two nuns and a cartload of baggage. After an exchange of smiles and hugs, the man followed the priest and the two nuns as they made their way to the security checkpoint.

Antonio and Pamela looked at each other and breathed a quiet sigh of relief.

★ ★ ★

'I have a plane to catch,' Schumann said. 'Before I go, I want to give you something, a small gift from an old man who still remembers the promise he made a long time ago.' He reached into a paper bag he was carrying, pulled out the antique music box and held it out for Elena.

'You didn't have to do that,' she said. She took the music box and placed it on her lap.

'Go ahead, open it,' he said, eager to see her reaction.

She gently opened the lid and out came the recognizable sounds of the *Blue Danube Waltz*. Smiling, she closed her eyes for a moment and moved her head to the rhythm of the music.

'I once promised to dance with you, Elena,' he said standing up with his hand extended. 'And today I would like to keep that promise. May I have this dance, Señorita?'

'You may,' she said giddily. She placed the music box on the couch, stood up, and took his hand.

They held each other at a proper distance and began to dance.

'You may not believe me but I used to be quite good at dancing the waltz,' he said. 'It was all part of being a well-bred gentleman.

An old world idea, I suppose. Nobody likes to waltz any more. It's considered too old-fashioned. Too bad. I think the world could use a little more Strauss and a little less noise.' He smiled. 'I'm beginning to sound like the old man that I am, aren't I?'

'No, you're not and you dance very well,' she said, trying to keep up with him.

They danced from one end of the room to the other and came to a stop in front of a window overlooking a small balcony.

'I'm beginning to feel like that girl you met so many years ago and I'm afraid,' she said, her voice quivering slightly.

'What are you afraid of?'

'I'm afraid of . . . ' She shook her head and tears trickled down her face.

Schumann stepped closer to her and reached to wipe her tears with his hand. 'It's time for me to go,' he said, fighting back his own tears.

She nodded and only mildly resisted when he moved closer and kissed her on the lips, at first gently and then passionately. They were in a tight embrace when the first shot rang out and a bullet crashed through the window and tore into his upper spine. He gave out a gasping sound and fell forward just as the second bullet hit him a little lower and came to rest inside Elena's heart. They fell to the floor, their arms still clutched around one another. The waltz played on for several more seconds until it slowed down and finally came to an end.

Across the street, behind a thick clump of bushes and tall trees, a man wearing khaki pants placed a high-powered rifle with a telescopic lens into a trombone case and calmly walked away from the area. When he was about half a mile away, he stepped up to a public telephone and made a long distance call.

'Hello?' Alfred said, sounding like he had been expecting the call.

'Your problem has been eliminated.'

'Good, we'll have your payment waiting for you as we agreed.'

★ ★ ★

Pamela looked at her watch. 'It's almost 10.30. If he were going to make the flight he would've been here by now.'

'Damn it! I should have stayed with him,' Antonio said, pounding his fist against his thigh. 'I believed him when he said he had a plane to catch.' His mind went over everything his father had said and he suddenly got up and bolted towards the nearest pay phone.

'Where are you going?' she said, getting up to follow him.

He ignored her as he stepped up to the phone and dialled his mother's number. He let it ring eight times but there was no answer.

He hung up, dialled Dr Pacheco's number and the housekeeper answered almost immediately.

'This is Antonio,' he said, rushing his words. 'Let me speak to Doctor Pacheco.'

'He left just minutes ago. He was in a hurry and didn't say where he was going.'

Antonio dropped the receiver. 'Let's get out of here,' he said, dashing out across the terminal.

★   ★   ★

When they got to his mother's apartment, Dr Pacheco was already there. He was sitting in a kneeling position with Elena's head resting against his knee.

'Elena, Elena,' he kept repeating. 'My dear Elena.'

They walked up to him and gently pulled him away from her. Trembling, Antonio returned to where his mother and father were lying and he stood over them for several moments. Then, when he heard the wailing of an ambulance fast approaching, he turned around and walked over to the couch. There was a small card on the floor and he picked it up and read it. It said:

I will love you forever,
Hans

Suddenly he was struck with the thought that someone had to decide what to do with his father's body.

'It's not fair!' he cried out, shaking his head. 'It's not fair!'

29

Sitting across from the funeral director, Antonio's mind kept wandering and he only half-listened to what the man was saying. 'Yes, that's fine,' he said numbly. 'Whatever you think is best.'

'And about the gentleman?' the funeral director asked. 'Do you want the same arrangements?'

Antonio looked at him as if he didn't understand the question. Why was it *his* responsibility? His father was a stranger to him. He felt a sudden rush of anger and he stood up and walked toward the door.

'Señor, you haven't told us what you want us to do with the body.'

'Do whatever you want with it,' he said, continuing to walk out of the office.

★   ★   ★

After listening to Antonio, Dr Pacheco walked over to the liquor cabinet and pulled out a bottle of brandy. He poured a small amount into a glass and handed it to Antonio. 'Take it. It's a little early in the day, but I

315

think you could use it.'

Antonio shook his head. 'Thanks, but I need to stay alert. I have a feeling it's going to be a long day.'

'Well, I certainly could use it,' Dr Pacheco said, downing the brandy in one gulp. 'You know what they're going to do, don't you? They're going to put his body in a common grave on top of a bunch of nameless people, no funeral, no prayers, no nothing. And if you want my opinion, that's exactly what he deserves. Stop worrying about it, Antonio. Legally, it's not your responsibility, and no one can force you to do otherwise.' He paused, still holding the empty glass. 'If I sound cold, it's because . . . ' His voice began to quiver. 'Because he destroyed all that I lived for.'

'Well, I know you probably want to be alone,' Antonio said. 'If I don't see you later today I'll see you tomorrow . . . at the funeral.'

Antonio left Dr Pacheco's house and took a cab to Pamela's hotel. When he entered the lobby, he saw her standing in front of the counter with her bags by her side.

'Where are you going?' he asked as he walked up to her.

'I didn't hear from you this morning and last night . . . well, I got the impression that you wanted to be left alone. Not that I blame you.'

'I was going to call you earlier but my phone wouldn't stop ringing,' he said. 'You've been there so you know what I'm talking about. Why don't we go into the coffee shop? I could use a strong cup right now. Just leave your bags there. I'm sure they'll be safe.'

The waitress seated them at a table that had an arrangement of freshly-cut flowers in a narrow, red vase set off to one side.

'Just coffee,' he said. The waitress pulled back the menus she was about to hand to them.

'My mother loved flowers,' he said staring at the vase. 'She especially loved carnations because they stayed fresh and full of color for a long time. I ordered three dozen of them along with some yellow roses.'

'I can only imagine what you're going through,' she said. 'Is there anything I can do to help?'

'It would mean a lot to me if you stayed, at least until after the funeral.'

'I'll unpack my bags,' she said with a reassuring smile. 'I can stay longer if you want me to.'

Antonio looked away for a second, the vivid scene from the night before still fresh in his mind. 'I'm sorry, what did you say?'

'I said that I'll stay as long you need me.'

'Thanks.'

'So what are you going to do?' she asked after the coffee had arrived.

'About my father?' He shook his head. 'I don't know. It's bad enough to have to plan my mother's funeral. But to be responsible for a stranger, a man who was never part of my life . . . it's just too much for me. I went to see Doctor Pacheco and he said I shouldn't worry about it because it wasn't my responsibility, legally or otherwise.'

'Maybe he's right. You really don't owe your father anything, and you shouldn't feel guilty about what happens to him.'

'I wish it were that simple. I can't change the fact that he was my father, and I can't help feeling I am responsible for what happens to him. If I don't tell the funeral director what to do with his body by the end of the day, they'll probably take care of it the way they do with other unclaimed bodies.'

'Well, would that be so bad?'

He thought about it for a moment. 'Probably not. I'm sure no one would even care. Anyway, I have the rest of the day to decide. I have to go back to my apartment to wait for some phonecalls. Want to come along?'

They stepped off the elevator just as Antonio's neighbors, a couple in their early sixties, were coming out of their apartment.

'We were so sorry to hear about your mother,' the man said, reaching out to shake Antonio's hand. 'Please accept our condolences. If there's anything we can do, just knock on our door.' Too choked up to say anything, the woman gave him a hug and turned away.

'Thank you. Thank you both,' Antonio said, not yet accustomed to accepting expressions of sympathy. He nodded to them and turned to walk the few steps to his apartment. He had the key in his hand when he looked down and saw the corner of a piece of paper that someone had slipped under the door. He reached down and pulled it out.

'What is it?' she asked.

He handed her the note. 'See for yourself.'

'Oh my God,' she said as she began to read it aloud. 'This is a warning to you. Your father was an evil man who did the devil's bidding and he must not be buried in holy ground. Take this warning seriously if you value your life.' She returned the note to him. 'This is unreal. Who could have done this?'

'I don't know. It could be almost anyone, a

Jew, a Catholic, anyone who is convinced that my father doesn't deserve a proper burial.'

'Maybe you should call the police.'

'And tell them what? I'm sure they have more important things to do than to worry about the veiled threats of some lunatic.'

'Is that what you think this is? How can you be sure? With everything that's happened I'd feel better if you'd take this a little more seriously.'

'All right,' he said in a yielding tone. 'I'll check it out. Look, I've a got a few things to do. Why don't you stay in my apartment and take the phonecalls? The funeral arrangements are on a piece of paper next to the phone. On my way out I'll check with the concierge to see if he saw anyone suspicious come up to this floor. I may be gone for a while, so make yourself at home. There's a half-empty bottle of wine and a few things in the refrigerator.'

★ ★ ★

Antonio sat in the rectory of St Cecilia Church, waiting for Father Quintana to arrive. Restless, he got up to make a phonecall.

'I'm at the rectory waiting for Father Quintana,' he said. 'Has anyone called?'

320

'Yes, a few of your mother's friends and also your secretary,' Pamela said. 'I gave them the information you left by the phone. There was one call that concerned me a little. After I gave him the information about the funeral, he wanted to know if the man who was killed was a relative.'

'Who was he?'

'Come to think of it, he didn't give his name. I told him that as far as I knew he was an old friend of your mother's.'

'Did he accept that?'

'Yes, but then he said, 'Tell Antonio to be careful', and he hung up.'

Antonio glanced over his shoulder and saw Father Quintana enter the rectory. 'I've got to go,' he said. 'Father Quintana just arrived. I'll talk to you later.' He hung up the phone and reached out to give Father Quintana a big hug.

'Thank you for coming,' Antonio said. 'Tomorrow is going to be a very difficult day for me and I feel better already knowing that you'll be there. I don't know what I would have done if you hadn't been able to make it.'

'I've been praying for you ever since you called,' Father Quintana said. 'Your mother is with our Lord Jesus Christ, with whom we will all be some day. Let's step in here.' They walked into a private office and sat down to talk — about the details of the funeral, at first, and later about the agonizing decision that Antonio felt had been unfairly placed on his shoulders.

An hour later they emerged from the office and after a quick goodbye, Antonio left the rectory and returned to his apartment.

He had a drained look on his face when he entered the living room and closed the door behind him.

Pamela was sitting on the couch. She got up and walked up to him.

'Are you all right?' she asked.

Antonio looked into her eyes and paused for a moment. 'No, not really,' he said in a half-whisper. 'I'm not sure I'm ready for tomorrow.'

'I know what you're going through. I only wish there was something I could do to make it easier. Did you decide about — '

'If you don't mind, I'd rather not talk about it. In fact for the rest of the day I'd like to put it all out of my mind. I just hope I can get some sleep tonight.'

'You shouldn't be alone. If you'd like I can spend the night.'

There was a short silence. 'I'd like that. I'd like that very much.' He moved closer to her and without even thinking, he leaned over and kissed her on the lips. She kissed him back and they held each other for several moments. Then the phone rang, and Antonio slowly broke away to answer it. It was another one of his mother's friends calling to express her sympathy.

★ ★ ★

Father Quintana's deep Castillian voice was clear and controlled as he read from the Book of Revelation.

'Behold God's dwelling is with the Human race. He will dwell with them and they will be his people, and God Himself will always be with them as their God. He will wipe every tear from their eyes, and there shall be no more death or mourning, wailing or pain, for the old order has passed away.' He looked at Antonio, then stepped up to Elena's casket and sprinkled holy water over it and blessed her. He did the same thing to the casket next to it, and when it was all over, he bowed his head in silence and then quietly turned to leave.

The words from his father's note still fresh in his mind, Antonio turned to Pamela. 'She would have wanted it this way,' he said mournfully. 'He loved her. He really did.'

Pamela nodded and held his hand tightly. 'It's time to go,' she said softly.

★ ★ ★

When the limousine in which they were riding was half a block away, Antonio glanced back through the rear window to catch a final glimpse, and saw an old man with a cane walk up to the grave site. He saw him lean over his father's casket and spit on it once, and then again.

Antonio turned back around in horror and tried to pretend that he hadn't seen anything.

'What's the matter?' Pamela asked.

'Nothing. It was nothing,' he said, a trace of tension in his voice. His mind reeled back to the beginning when he first met Harry Friedman and he suddenly realized that it wasn't really over. The pain and the rage would continue for still a few more years until there would be no more Schumanns left to hate, no more Friedmans left to cry for.

THE END

We do hope that you have enjoyed reading this large print book.

Did you know that all of our titles are available for purchase?

We publish a wide range of high quality large print books including:
Romances, Mysteries, Classics
General Fiction
Non Fiction and Westerns

Special interest titles available in large print are:
The Little Oxford Dictionary
Music Book
Song Book
Hymn Book
Service Book

Also available from us courtesy of Oxford University Press:
Young Readers' Dictionary
(large print edition)
Young Readers' Thesaurus
(large print edition)

For further information or a free brochure, please contact us at:
Ulverscroft Large Print Books Ltd.,
The Green, Bradgate Road, Anstey,
Leicester, LE7 7FU, England.
Tel: (00 44) **0116 236 4325**
Fax: (00 44) **0116 234 0205**

Other titles in the
Ulverscroft Large Print Series:

THE FROZEN CEILING

Rona Randall

When Tessa Pickard found the note amongst her father's possessions, instinct told her that THIS had been responsible for his suicide, not the professional disgrace which had ruined his career as a mountaineer and instructor. The note was cryptic, anonymous, and bore a Norwegian postmark. Tessa promptly set out for Norway, determined to trace the anonymous letter-writer, but unprepared for the drama she was to uncover — or that compelling Max Hyerdal, whom she met on board a Norwegian ship, was to change her whole life.

GHOSTMAN

Kenneth Royce

Jones boasted that he never forgot a face. When he was found dead outside the National Gallery it was assumed he had remembered one too many. The man he had claimed to have identified had been publicly executed in Moscow some years before. The presumed look-alike was called Mirek and his background stood up. The Security Service calls in Willie 'Glasshouse' Jackson — Jacko — as they realise that there is a more sinister aspect. Jacko and his assistant begin to unearth commercial and political corruption in which life is cheap and profits vast, as the killing machines swing into action.

THE READER

Bernhard Schlink

A schoolboy in post-war Germany, Michael collapses one day in the street and is helped home by a woman in her thirties. He is fascinated by this older woman, and he and Hanna begin a secretive affair. Gradually, he begins to be frustrated by their relationship, but then is shocked when Hanna simply disappears. Some years later, as a law student, Michael is in court to follow a case. To his amazement he recognizes Hanna. The object of his adolescent passion is a criminal. Suddenly, Michael understands that her behaviour, both now and in the past, conceals a deeply buried secret.